PRAISE FOR MA

"Matt Kurtz is a fresh voice of horror, one that screams in your head with the intensity of a revving chainsaw. When it comes to scaring readers, the man is a natural, and that just makes his work all the more frightening."
—**Kristopher Triana**
author of *Gone to See the River Man* and *Full Brutal*

"Kurtz's use of language and description is so magical that we are almost lost within the beauty of word choice to notice someone has had their brains splattered against the wall."
—**Ginger Nuts of Horror**

KINFOLK

"…an all-out gory smackdown fight to the finish… If you're looking for quiet, elevated, or literary horror, this is not the book for you." —**The Horror Fiction Review**

"A fast-moving tale of survival…exciting and addictive."
—**Red Lace Reviews**

"…it's not for the faint of heart. From the jump, it's nonstop mayhem and savagery." —**Cedar Hollow Horror Reviews**

"From the very first moment until the last blood-soaked scene, you will be left breathless." —**Ginger Nuts of Horror**

"…an entertaining and fast-moving white-knuckle ride…"
—**Horror DNA**

"…a high-octane thrill ride that is violent, shocking, and grim without losing its playful nature." —**Library Macabre**

"Intense, brutal, and bloody…" —**Sci-Fi & Scary**

THE ROTTING WITHIN

"…heartbreaking, disturbing, and scary as hell."
—**ScareTissue.com**

"…gripping from start to finish…" —**HorrorFuel.com**

"THIS is how you write a damn supernatural horror novel." —**Uptown Horror Reviews**

"The creepiness factor is off the charts…"
—**Horror Bookworm Reviews**

"Tense, scary, and unpredictable, with a killer ending… Highly recommended." —**IndieMuse.com**

"Unsettling from the onset..." —**Red Lace Reviews**

"Filled with heart-pounding jump-scares, nerve-shredding dread, and an ending that will shock and disturb you…"
—**TheLineUp.com**

"This one was a hell of a ride: fast-paced, action-packed, descriptively immersive, gory, cinematic, and actually scary, with an absolute gut punch of an ending."
—**ScareSalon.com**

"With a masterful use of tension building…and a startling ending that will leave your jaw on the floor, *The Rotting Within* did not disappoint." —**The Wandering Reader**

ALSO BY MATT KURTZ

NOVELS
The Rotting Within
Kinfolk

SHORT STORY COLLECTIONS
Monkey's Box of Horrors
Monkey's Bucket of Horrors
Monkey's Butcher Block of Horrors

Shock Waves
Copyright © 2023 Matt Kurtz
All rights reserved.

Front cover designed and illustrated by Chelsea Lowe
cmloweart.com

"Big Mama" (Scorpion-Mantis) illustration by Alfi Neizear

Edited by 360 Editing (a division of Uncomfortably Dark Horror)
Editors: Candace Nola and Darcy Rose

Cover wrap from Squidbar Designs

Umbra Press logo designed by Gary McCluskey

ISBN: 9798377005629

This is a work of fiction. All characters and events portrayed in this book are fictitious and any resemblance to real people, places, or events is purely coincidental.

No part of this book may be reproduced, stored in a retrieval system, or transmitted in any form or by any means, including mechanical, electric, photocopying, recording, or otherwise, without the prior written permission of the publisher or author.

SHOCK WAVES

MATT KURTZ

UMBRA
PRESS

Special thanks to C.V. Hunt, Ashley Saywers,
Kristopher Triana, John Wayne Comunale, Alicia Stamps,
and Scott Kurtz.

ONE

SATURDAY, SEPTEMBER 3RD, 1988
8:49PM

AS THE STORM CREPT closer, it was business as usual at The Lone Star Land Amusement Park.

I helped guests from their seats and ushered them to the exit, clearing the train for the next batch of riders. After the train was reloaded, locked down, and zipping out of the station, I returned to check on the ominous clouds rolling our way.

Our ride, Shock Waves, was an all-steel roller coaster with triple loops that flipped passengers upside down and sideways. It was one of the most popular attractions in the park, and I was proud to be its foreman at only seventeen years old.

My crew consisted of a dozen other teenagers, whose main responsibilities were loading and unloading trains, as well as guest safety. To keep things fresh, we rotated the various positions at the top of every hour.

Greg, my night-shift assistant foreman, dispatched behind a control panel of blinking lights. The gawky, seventeen-year-old with braces was my backup driver, which allowed me to take a dinner break earlier. Normally, I would be dispatching for the rest of the night, but I wanted to give him more time "behind the wheel" so he could get promoted to foreman of his own ride next season.

After eyeing the dark band of clouds, Greg stated the obvious. "You think we got a storm heading our way?"

I stared at him and nearly said, "Really, dude?" but opted to remain silent. After the argument I had with Stacy on break, there was no reason to rip on Greg.

Actually, Stacy and I didn't really argue. I was just being an insensitive dickhead about an issue troubling us. My words caused her to tear up, leave the table, and head back to her ride without saying goodbye, let alone "I love you."

In the hour that passed, I'd come to my senses and regretted not necessarily what was said, but how I said it. Our dinner break at work wasn't the time or place for such a discussion.

Now, I owed her an apology when we got off in a few hours, that's if she didn't cut out early and ditch me altogether. If that were the case, I wouldn't be able to talk to her until tomorrow morning since her parents had a strict policy of no phone calls after ten.

I trudged up the control booth steps, plopped down on the driver's bench next to Greg, and, once again, peered at the strobing clouds over his shoulder.

"Think we'll close early?" Greg asked.

"Hope so."

We had three hours left until closing. If it rained, it would take at least that long for the track to dry out. Management would most likely cut its losses and shut down the park early, opting to send everyone home rather than keep a bunch of closed rides fully staffed.

That call couldn't come soon enough.

I glanced at the park phone mounted next to us.

"What time is it, anyway?"

Greg checked his wristwatch, or, as we called it, his shackle. It had a watchband that was a three-inch wide leather cuff secured by a buckle on the underside. A real hippy looking thing.

"Five to nine," he said.

I sighed. The sooner we shut down, the sooner I could make things right with Stacy. It sucked knowing she was out there mad at me, and because of it, I could already tell it was going to be one hell of a long night.

TWO

THUNDER RUMBLED IN THE distance. We eyed the dark horizon consuming the purple sky. At the very least, we should've been getting a call about lightning (which, even without the rain, was enough to temporarily shut us down.)

"About time for rotations?" Greg said while monitoring the lights on the control panel.

"Yeah, once Kyra gets back from break. Which should be—"

She was already walking up the exit ramp toward us.

Kyra was a few months shy of seventeen. Dark ebony skin, athletic build, sharp as a tack, and one kick-ass personality to boot. I considered setting up my kid brother Mick with her but thought better. Although they were about the same age, she was too good for him. And even if I did, I was afraid Mick might cave to peer pressure from his dipshit friends about dating a black chick and ruin something good.

Kyra was an awesome employee. Hard worker. Always early to her shift. Would change a trash can or tidy up the queue line without being asked. She was great with the guests, always greeting them with a genuine smile, yet stern when they tried something stupid. I already told my supervisors that if she returned next season, I wanted her as my assistant foreman.

"Ready for rotations?" she asked before I could.

"Yeah."

"You get my Snickers?" Greg said.

Kyra held up the candy bar. "Think fast!" She did a cartwheel, and on the way up, tossed him the snack.

Greg caught it with one hand.

"Nice!" Kyra said.

"You too. Your form looks great."

"Thanks, dude!" She bounded up the steps of the booth, sandwiching me between them. "Slap me cinco."

They high-fived over me.

"Don't you have that big meet coming up?" I said.

"I do! The twenty-fourth. Pleeeease remember not to schedule me that day. Or it'll be the first time I ever call in sick."

"Don't worry. I got you covered." I looked down and picked out dirt from under my fingernail. "Ya know, I really wish me and Stacy could be there for you. We feel bad about it, but you know how hard it is for me to take off on Saturdays around here. I wish there was something I could do."

(Boy, I was laying it on thick. I'd already cleared it with my supervisor to leave work early that day. There was no way Stacy and I were going to miss Kyra's gymnastics meet. We knew how much it meant to her and planned to show up with a bouquet, then cheer her on so loudly she'd probably die of embarrassment.)

She meekly shrugged. "It's okay. There'll be other meets."

"Yeah," Greg said. "I need to check one out sometime. Especially with all those hot gymnast chicks in their tight, skimpy outfits."

Kyra gave him a look. "Skimpy outfits? You ever been to the beach or a swimming pool? You'll see more skin there."

"I guess. But then, how would I know? Working all these long hours puts a real crimp in my social life."

Kyra and I exchanged a glance. Greg had no social life, but we didn't call him out on it.

In fact, most park employees didn't have one, and it had nothing to do with long hours on the job. The simple fact was, in the 'real' world, we were a bunch of outsiders. We were the math nerds, choir and band geeks, drama dweebs, wallflowers, bookworms, freaks, headbangers, new wavers, skaters, exchange students, and all-around loners from about a half dozen surrounding high schools that united into one inclusive group at the park.

We rarely saw a prep, jock, or popular kid come looking for employment there. Most didn't need a job because they got allowances or their parents bought them everything. To them, summers meant a three-month vacation where they could sleep in 'til noon. To us, it was an opportunity to work full time and save up some money.

In many ways, the place was another high school, only for misfits. Everyone was accepted. I guess you could say the park *was* our social life, so much so that a lot of the employees, once their shift ended, changed out of uniform and hung out, riding rides, and socializing with other crews.

Kyra and I exited the booth to leave Greg alone with his Snickers. We paused at the bottom step to review our rotation schedule on the clipboard.

"Hey," Greg said with caramel and nougat all stuck in his braces. "They have the weather on in the canteen?"

Kyra nodded. "It's supposed to get hairy. Surprised they haven't already shut us down for lightning." She paused and thumbed back to the coaster. "Any more complaints since I was gone?"

Hours earlier, a couple of guests informed us how jarring it was coming out of the side loop, more so than usual. A single complaint usually gets chalked up to someone being overly dramatic, but more people mentioned it while Kyra was on break.

"Two others," I answered. "Once rotations are done, I'll hop in for a ride and see for myself. Hopefully, we won't have to call maintenance."

"Oh, crap!" Kyra said. "Billy's working tonight."

"Yep, he's the mechanic on duty," I said. "So, let's hope it's nothing."

Kyra sighed and pointed at her white, pristine tennis shoes. "Man, I just got these. You remember the last time he was called here?"

How could I forget?

She reminded me anyway. "He spit his nasty-ass tobacco juice all over my other shoes. Didn't even apologize, either. Just said I shouldn't have been standing there."

"I know. But think of it this way, if he comes out and finds something, we might close even earlier."

"Or they'll make us wait while he farts around with things," Greg said. "Can we just act like no one complained, wait for the rain to hit, and let dayshift handle things in the morning?"

"No," I said, and my tone meant it wasn't open for discussion.

"Okay, rotation-wise, what am I doing next? Taking your place unloading?"

"Yes, ma'am. Then I replace Stan over on loading. He goes down to the lift and replaces Deb. She comes up, takes my place, and then I go for a ride to determine whether we need to call your buddy Billy."

Kyra rolled her eyes.

I shared her lack of enthusiasm for the man. Billy could be quite intimidating. Physically, he was a cross between a lumberjack and a linebacker. Although I don't think he even knew my name, I was the only one he came to about maintenance issues, being the foreman and all. Occasionally, I stuttered and stammered when trying to explain the problem, especially if I caught my puny, distorted reflection in his black eyes. Over time, I realized the less flowery the description, the better he responded.

"Billy. Thump-thump. Bottom of second loop. Rough ride. Paaaaainnnnnn." Then off he'd go to investigate. I was already thinking about how to streamline our current situation in case his expertise was needed tonight.

Farther down, the rising pneumatic brakes let off a loud hiss, then the incoming train screeched to a halt outside the station.

Once it stopped there, the driver resumed control and carefully guided it in, pumping the air brakes along the track to slow or speed up its reentry.

Only now it wasn't moving, which was a cause for concern.

THREE

WE TURNED TO SEE WHY Greg wasn't bringing in the train. He stood over the control panel and threw his hands in the air, giving us a *'Don't look at me'* response. He pointed to our loader, Stan, a lanky seventeen-year-old with freckles, braces, and red hair that was prematurely thinning.

Stan should've been in position on the opposite side of the station, pressing a button to allow the train in. It was a two-person safety setup, so a driver couldn't bring in a train unless the loader confirmed all guests were safely inside their stalls.

Instead of doing his job, Stan flirted with two girls next in line to ride.

With a deep trough and track separating our side of the platform from his, our only way to get his attention was to yell across. Greg screamed his name, but it was drowned out by the crowd noise and the blaring music on the park's stereo system.

Before Kyra or I could shout over, Greg wadded up a piece of paper from the clipboard and chucked it at Stan.

The paper ball bounced off the back of his head.

Although some witnesses gawked and giggled at the accuracy of the shot, the two girls Stan was busting a move on laughed at him.

Mortified, he spun to see who was responsible. His acne-riddled face turned beet red, accenting his whiteheads even more.

Greg waved and gave a shit-eating grin.

With his hands clenched into fists, Stan glared at Greg from the opposite side of the trough. "What's your damage, dude?!"

I stepped between my two crew members locked in a standoff.

"C'mon, Stan," I said. "Move your ass. You're holding up the entire ride." I pointed to the button at the far end of the station for him to push.

He begrudgingly did as he was told.

The train rolled forward. With a deafening hiss from the pneumatic brakes, it slid to a stop in front of us.

I moved to the middle of the train while Kyra positioned herself at its front. Like flight attendants, we instructed the guests (motioning in unison) how to unlock their lap bars and leave the ride.

"Push down, lift up, and exit to your right."

"Your other right, sir," Kyra said to the man exiting to his left.

There was one on every train. Once the guy's confusion turned to slight embarrassment, Kyra warmly smiled and motioned for him to move with the rest of the crowd. He crossed through an empty car, rejoined his herd, and followed everyone down the exit ramp.

Before the gates opened and ushered in the next set of riders, I crossed through the empty train to the other side and approached Stan, who was sulking by the button.

The pneumatic gates opened with a hiss behind me, unleashing guests to storm the train.

"Dude, that was a dick move," Stan said, obviously referring to the paper ball incident. "Greg is totally cruisin' for a bruisin' if he keeps that crap up."

"Agreed. It was uncalled for, and I'll talk to him about it later. But we were only trying to get your attention."

Ironically, his attention was already waning.

"Yeah-yeah. Do what now?"

The girls he was flirting with earlier had settled into their seats and lowered their lap bars in anticipation of the ride.

"Hey-ah, just give me a sec. Gotta make sure those babes are safe and secure, if you know what I mean."

When he stepped toward the ladies, I planted a hand on his chest.

"Nuh-uh. Time for rotations. I'm taking your place loading." I pointed in the opposite direction, at the descending stairs. "Go down to the lift and—"

"The lift?! Oh, c'mon! Don't cockblock me like this!"

"I'm not. If those girls come back looking for you, I'll tell them you'll return in an hour. But with the storm that's coming, I'm sure you'll be back up here in thirty minutes or so."

"Dude! This *so* totally bites the big one."

"Everyone's worked lift tonight except you. It's your turn. It's only fair."

"Yeah-yeah. Whatever."

"Now, go. Replace Deb so she can come up and take my place. And grab a raincoat from below. Just in case."

Stan trudged down the stairs with all the enthusiasm of a man being led to the gallows.

I never understood why everyone hated working the lift. It involved nothing physical, just watching a train get pulled up the first hill and looking for anyone trying to wiggle out from under their lap bar (Darwinism at its best.)

On the rare occasion a train got stuck on the lift, it was the responsibility of the lift operator to go uphill (via a catwalk) and babysit the guests. Keep them calm until the ride resumed. Other than those two things, it was basically standing around, daydreaming for an hour.

After Stan disappeared down the stairs, it took three ride cycles before Deb came up. As usual, she made sure to take her time during rotations. Anything to avoid having to work the full hour.

Although she could be difficult, I tried to cut her some slack. I'd seen the bruised handprints on her arms and knew there was trouble at home. My suspicions were confirmed the first time I gave her a ride home after work. She told me to drop her off at the end of her street and she'd walk the rest of the way. Because it was well after midnight and she lived with her dad on the shitty side of town, I objected and told her I'd drive up to her front curb. She went bug-eyed and grabbed my arm with a death grip.

"No! It's easier on me if he doesn't know who gave me a ride home. Especially if it's a boy. Trust me."

After seeing the fear in her eyes, I respected her wishes, and from then on, tried not to be too hard on her. I think while at work, she did things at her own pace because she sure as hell couldn't do it at home.

When Deb finally appeared on the top landing of the stairs, she moseyed over to take my place.

"How nice of you to join us," Kyra yelled over the trough at her. "You get lost or something?"

Deb glared at Kyra, her eyes narrowing behind her thick coke-bottle glasses. Both ladies squared off across the track. The ground shook. If not for the approaching train, I'd swear it could've been from the growing tension between them.

Knowing Deb was prone to curse like a sailor in front of guests, I figured it was best to de-escalate things.

"Deb, hit the button, would ya?"

Instead of doing what I asked, she sneered at me and

glared back at Kyra.

Greg waited at the control panel for someone—anyone—to hit the damn button.

"C'mon, guys," I said. "Everyone chill. Deb, bring in the train. Now."

She finally did, and we all yelled, "Push down, lift up, and exit to your right," which was immediately followed by, "No, your other right."

With the train only about half full, and most of the guests sitting up front, I hopped in the second to the last seat for my ride inspection.

I took a quick note of the surrounding passengers. Behind me was a Hispanic couple in their mid-twenties. I noticed them earlier in line because of their western apparel. She wore bright turquoise ropers. He had on a ball cap and one of those gigantic cowboy belt buckles that made him look like a WWF champion. A few seats up, a middle-aged woman sat alone. Her sunburned face was beet red, except for the pale area in the shape of oversized sunglasses.

Once everyone settled, Greg closed the pneumatic stalls while Deb and Kyra ran up and down the train, quickly tugging on the lap bars to ensure they were locked. Both women raised an index finger at Greg, signaling all was clear. Then the air brakes lowered with a loud hiss, and we rolled forward. After the train left the station and hit the base of the hill, the spinning lift chain hooked into the first car—then each consecutive car after that—and we were slowly pulled up the steep incline.

Little did I know, most of us wouldn't make it off the hill alive.

FOUR

NERVOUS LAUGHTER AND CHEERS of excitement swelled from both ends of the train. As we inched higher and cleared the northern perimeter fence, I slid across the seat and stared past the interstate parallel to us.

Beyond the highway was a large construction site that operated twenty-four-seven. Whatever the Penumbra Construction Co. was building—apartments, a mall, an office complex—they must've been on an extremely tight schedule. I'd recently pulled more than a few doubles at the park, and their bulldozers, dump trucks, and excavators hustled like a colony of ants from when I arrived at seven AM until well past midnight.

In less than a week, an overgrown field became a stripped plot of earth with a large hole carved out of its center.

As the sky grew from purple to black, huge work lights flooded the site. Oddly enough, it appeared they had no intention of stopping for the storm, which would put them at risk of being struck by lightning or turning the area into a gigantic mud pit.

When the rear of the train hit the middle of the incline, it cleared the treetops to my left and revealed the neighboring ride.

Stacy's ride.

I quickly slid over to see if I could spot her working on the dock of The Rip-Roaring Rapids.

The attraction simulated a white-water rafting adventure, where a dozen guests were belted into an inner tube-like boat and whisked through a turbulent, man-made river lined with rock face walls.

Stacy wasn't on the dock, so I searched the area behind it, hidden from the public while at ground level.

Then I spotted her, and my heart leapt with excitement.

She strolled down a well-lit, tree-lined walkway to their SPs—or safety posts, which were sentry stands positioned along the ride to make sure passengers remained seated.

Their SPs were the equivalent of our lift position. At our ride, any idiotic guest that escaped from their lap bar could fall to their death. At hers, they could drown.

The train continued uphill, and a second later, Stacy was gone, gobbled up by the Rapids' dense foliage.

I faced forward and gazed at the headrest of the empty seat in front of me.

My thoughts fell to our future, and a familiar knot of dread pulled tighter in my belly.

In a matter of months, our lives would change forever.

Unfortunately, not for the better.

Stacy and I had been exclusive for nearly two years. Like most teens, we had a very active sex life. Although abstinence was expected, it certainly wasn't practiced, not when it came to the raging hormones of a teenager. On the rare occasion a condom wasn't available, we used the pull-out method. The last time we did that was a little over a month and a half ago.

We figured that's when it happened.

When she missed her period, we knew we were in trouble. At first, we remained in denial, thinking it could never happen to us. (Hell, we'd only graduated high school a few months ago.) We just had to wait and see if she'd have it next month. Sometimes women can skip a period. Or so we heard.

Then a few days ago, unbeknownst to me, Stacy grew impatient and had a friend buy her an early pregnancy test. The results confirmed what we'd been fearing.

We were going to be teenage parents.

When she told me, I heard what she said, but it still took a few minutes to process it. This shit was really happening. Once I realized that, I couldn't breathe and slumped in my car seat. We held each other and cried, terrified of our future and dreading how everyone, especially our parents, would react to the news.

I had to start looking for a *real* job. No more working at an amusement park. Worst-case scenario, when I turned eighteen in less than two months, I could join something like the National Guard for the extra pay and benefits. Or were they strictly volunteer? (The only thing I knew about them was they had an armory close by, near downtown, that was a big tourist attraction.)

For now, we could kiss our chances of going to college goodbye since we'd have to use that money to survive.

What a mess.

Inhaling sharply, I smelled the electricity in the air and glanced ahead. The approaching clouds strobed across the black sky as lightning ricocheted within their cottony mass. Things were about to get hairy, but if it meant closing early so I could apologize to Stacy about my *suggestion* to her earlier in the canteen, then maybe some higher power was looking out for—

Something exploded. Deafening and to my right.

I leaped from my seat until my lap bar threw me back down. Then the shock wave from the blast slammed me against the far side of the car.

The explosion came from the construction site across the highway.

Terrified screams erupted around me.

The front of the train, which had already made it over the hill and onto the track, swayed to the left, while we remained stationary.

The metal support beams groaned under the strain.

If the cars didn't stretch and rip apart, they would pull us off the side of the hill.

After an excruciatingly long moment, the front half of the train slowly shifted back into place, aligning with the rear.

Then the world around us stopped.

FIVE

ONCE THE REVERB FROM the explosion faded into the distance, the lights around us flickered, and the amusement park plunged into darkness.

The clicking chain pulling us up the hill died, and the train halted. The ride's air horn bellowed once for three seconds, signaling a train was stuck on the lift. Numerous other horns went off around the park, telling the same story for different rides.

The highway traffic between the park and the construction site crawled to a stop, either from the accidents caused by the blast or rubberneckers hoping to catch sight of a little carnage. Some drivers laid on their horns to get traffic flowing again. Thankfully, the headlights along the highway provided enough illumination to see, but the rest of the park, including most of our station house below, was erased from sight.

Beneath the train, the coaster's track creaked again. I squeezed the lap bar white-knuckle tight, waiting for the hill to crumble, but it remained intact, and we didn't plunge to our deaths.

Once able to breathe again, I peered at the construction site to see what happened.

A thick veil of dust concealed the entire area. After a few moments, the brown haze swirled and was blown away by an icy wind from the incoming storm.

The headlights of various construction vehicles showcased the damage. An excavator lay on its side like a dying dinosaur. Workers, caked in dirt, stumbled around in a daze while others exited their damaged vehicles.

A long fissure, at least ten feet wide, zig-zagged across the ground, splitting the work site in two.

Over my shoulder, the park remained in complete darkness. I don't know why I expected anything different, but the sight was still surreal. As was the silence. The usual cacophony of roaring rides, laughter, cheers of excitement, and the park's sound system playing Creedence Clearwater Revival's "I Heard It Through the Grapevine" (for the zillionth time) was replaced by calls for help echoing out of an abyss. I tried to spot Stacy again, but the blackness swallowed her ride.

Still clutching the lap bar with a death grip, I faced forward and sank in my seat.

They must have hit a gas line while digging. Whatever it was, blew the power grid the park was on. Miles away, lights were visible along the horizon, but nothing in the immediate vicinity.

A frigid breeze blew in as a reminder of the approaching storm. As did the ominous rumble of thunder.

Time to get back on the clock.

I looked past the empty seats in front of me and saw that the next car up (the one containing the woman with the raccoon sunburn) was stuck on the crest of the hill. With our car being the last one still hooked to the lift chain, it anchored the rest of the train, keeping everyone hanging there and preventing them from dropping into the first loop.

It was a terrible spot to be stuck.

"Hello?!" a voice from the front of the train called out.

"We're stuck!"

No duh.

"Somebody?!" "Anybody?!"

"Help!"

I tested my lap bar again to make sure it was locked. Although it provided peace of mind that I wouldn't fall out, it also confirmed I was trapped like everyone else.

I wondered how my crew was handling things below and strained to look down the hill. Leaning out a little more, I checked for Stan at the lift position. He should've been heading our way.

"Help!! We're stuck up here!" came from the front of the train.

"Oh, for Pete's sake! Turn the ride back on!"

With still no sign of Stan, I yelled ahead, "Help is on the way! Everybody, please relax!"

"Who said that?" a woman said from up front. "How do you know it's coming?!"

"Because I'm the…" I suddenly realized how bad it would sound saying I was the ride foreman and was stuck there with the rest of them. "Just… because!"

Searching for Stan again, I locked eyes with the Hispanic couple behind me. They smiled politely, then observed my park uniform and employee name tag. The woman opened her mouth to speak, but a clap of thunder stole her words.

The man ticked his head at the strobing storm clouds closing in.

"Hey, chief," he said. "You gonna get us out of here before that hits?"

"Uhhh…" *Choose your words carefully.* "Unfortunately, *I* can't. I'm trapped here…" I winced. "I'm *in* here just like you guys. But someone is on the way." I searched again for Stan.

The woman watched me and said, "You sure about that?"

"Oh, yeah. Absolutely. We have a position specifically for situations like this."

"Then where are they?"

"Well... um..."

Radio crackle came from out of the darkness. *"Stan..."* Kyra said. Her voice was thin and tinny. *"Are you there yet? Over."*

Farther down the catwalk, we saw movement within the void, then lightning flashed to reveal Stan slowly walking up the hill. One hand gripped the side railing; the other held a walkie-talkie to his mouth.

"I'm moving as fast as I can," he said, responding to Kyra. "Don't have a cow!"

After taking his sweet-ass time, Stan approached my car and pointed at me. "Ha. Sucks to be you."

He hooked an arm around the railing, leaned over, and shoved the walkie at me. "Here. Hold this."

Befuddled, I did what was asked while he dug in his pocket. A moment later, he produced the key to unlock the lap bars manually.

The instrument was more of a tool than your standard key. It was a grooved, four-inch, metal pin with a plastic ball on one end. Although I was proud he remembered to bring it, park protocol required that a supervisor and a mechanic be present whenever unlocking a lap bar after the train leaves the station. Which was why it confused me when he crouched beside my car and inserted the key into the slot.

"Stan? What are you doing?!"

"Getting you out so you can take it from here." He unlocked my lap bar and pulled it up.

I slammed it back down until it clicked and relocked.

"Whoa! You can't do this."

"Why not?"

"Because a supe has to be here when unloading someone. Even me. Otherwise, you'll get fired. You know this."

The guy behind me waved for Stan to come closer.

"Hey. Stan? I'm Juan. And this here," he pointed to the woman beside him, "is Lidia, my wife. You can let *us* out. We'll go."

Lidia nodded. "C'mon, Stan. Let us out. If he doesn't want to go, we'll be happy to."

"Sorry," I said. "But no one can leave the train until it's cleared by a supervisor and a mechanic. It's protocol because of the risk involved."

"Risk?" a woman said from over my shoulder. "You wanna talk risk?" It was the sunburned lady with the inverted racoon eyes sitting three seats up. "How about being up here when the storm hits? We can get struck by lightning. I mean, for Pete's sake, we're sitting ducks."

"Totally," Stan said.

I wanted to kill him for agreeing but couldn't blame the guy for doing so. I sure as hell wanted out myself, but Stan and I would get our asses fired for unloading anyone not in immediate danger. We weren't at that point yet, but a supe had better get there pretty darn quick. Unfortunately, there were only four of them on duty, each responsible for the rides in their assigned quadrant of the park. Under normal circumstances, if something went down, they would be there within five minutes. But if *all* the rides stopped at once? That was trouble.

The sky rumbled and the clouds lit up, mocking my concerns.

Although I was trapped on the train, I still had to appear in charge.

"A supervisor and a mechanic are on the way," I told

whoever was within earshot. "We'll be out of here shortly."

I returned to Stan. "Go up there and talk to the rest of the train and put them at ease."

"Talk to them? About what?"

"About how we'll be down shortly."

"Will we?"

"Yes! Now do it."

Stan stared ahead and craned his neck from side to side. "Dude, there's like half a car before the catwalk ends. The rest of the train is already way out on the freakin' track."

"Then go to the end of the catwalk and yell to them. They need to know someone from the ride is present."

"Um… then why didn't you do that earlier when you were just sitting here?"

"I did. Sort of."

Stan leaned in, finally showing a little self-awareness about being in uniform. "Dude, this is bullshit. I really don't wanna talk to these—"

Tremors rocked the coaster.

As the track swayed, its metal groaned, which ushered in a fresh wave of screams from all aboard.

During the chaos, Stan lost his balance. While reaching for something to hold on to, he dropped the lap bar key into my car.

He stumbled away, closer to the edge of the catwalk. I grabbed him by his shirt and reeled him back in. Another set of hands sprung from the seat behind me to help secure him.

Once the vibrations subsided and the roller coaster went still, Juan and I slowly let him go.

Stan's eyes bulged in terror.

"Oh, fuck y'all. I'm sooo outta here! Good luck with all this!"

Then he started down the catwalk.

SIX

"STAN! WAIT!"

"Amigo!" Juan said. "Don't leave us here!"

Lightning flashed again, and Stan abruptly halted.

"Oh, no," he said. "Great! Just great!" He turned and retreated up the hill, back to us.

We leaned out of the car and spotted the reason behind his sudden change of heart.

With a heavy-duty Maglite tucked under one beefy arm, a beast of a man ascended the slope. His body mass consumed the narrow catwalk, making it impossible for Stan to pass. Lightning strobed to reveal his flattop haircut, thick Winnfield mustache, and blue Dickies uniform. With each step, the gigantic wrenches dangling from his leather work belt swayed like the pendulum on a grandfather clock. Their movement and weight would easily throw off-balance any mere mortal. But not Billy. Oh, no. Continuing upward, the mechanic kept both hands free of the railing so he could pinch a hefty wad of loose-leaf chewing tobacco from a crinkled pouch.

Stan fled until cornering himself at the end of the catwalk.

Billy followed him. Without a hint of acknowledgement, he peered over the cowering young man pinned against the railing.

He surveyed the train on the track, then our section still attached to the lift chain. He grunted. Crouched and peeked under the car with his flashlight. Then rose. We silently watched the imposing figure. Billy grunted again, looked down at me, and did a double take.

I gulped.

"What the hell are you doing in there?" Without taking his eyes off me, Billy whipped his head to the side and spit a stream of tobacco juice, not giving two shits where it landed.

The warm, brown fluid splashed Stan's bare legs and seeped into his socks, soiling them. The teen flinched and whimpered.

"I was doing a safety check when something exploded across the highway. Then the power went out."

Billy's eyes darted to the construction site.

"Safety checks are supposed to be done at shift change. Not five hours into it."

"I did it then. But the last hour, people complained about how bumpy it was coming out of the side loop. So, I was going for a ride to see for myself."

Billy's attention shifted to the highway. "What a goddamn mess. Such fuckin' impatient people."

I winced at his language, only because there were guests around.

Then he double downed, screaming at the motorists, "Like honking your horn is gonna clear traffic any faster, assholes!" He shook his head, grunted, and addressed me. "Next time you get a complaint like that, you call me."

"Oh, of course. But until I knew there was a problem, I didn't want you to come out and waste your time."

"If there's a bunch of complaints, there's usually something to it, Danny."

Holy crap! Billy knew my name! (And he didn't even

look at my name tag.)

"If you even *think* there's a problem," Billy continued, "you call me. Get it?"

"Got it."

"Good."

Then Billy addressed the rest of the train. "All right, folks. We'll have you down and safely on the ground before the storm hits. Just sit tight, relax, and enjoy the view."

He whipped the flashlight over to Stan and blinded him with it.

"You! Zit Face! Get over here and hold this light."

Stan nodded and inched closer to the man as if approaching a rabid dog. Billy shoved the flashlight into his hand, then both crouched on the walkway to inspect something below.

Suddenly, the roller coaster shook so hard my vision blurred and my face went numb. I clutched the lap bar and my knuckles turned to chalk.

Billy and Stan dove for the train to avoid falling off the catwalk. I grabbed an arm for each man, then pulled them halfway into the car with me.

Lidia and Juan reached through the headrests and helped hold the men down. While Stan sniveled and screamed, Billy pointed at the construction site.

"Holy shit-balls!" he said.

I turned, and my eyes widened in terror.

SEVEN

THE DIVIDED EARTH SHIFTED again and dropped away, doubling the width of the original fissure.

Another explosion came from underground, then a gigantic wave of dirt blasted out of the opening.

Large chunks of debris rocketed into the night sky and disappeared into the low hanging storm clouds. I held my breath and prayed their trajectory wouldn't send them crashing down upon us.

The rumbling earth slowed to a stop. As the dust settled, an eerie stillness fell over the area. The spectacle even silenced the honking horns along the interstate.

"*Danny!*" Kyra's voice leaped out of Stan's walkie-talkie, causing us all to jump. "*You guys okay up there?! Over.*"

I'd forgotten all about Stan's radio. I felt around the floorboard and snatched it up.

"Yeah. We're okay. How about you guys? Over."

"*We're good.*"

"Are the supes on the way?"

"*Don't know. I can't call Operations. Our phone is dead.*"

A collective groan came from all within earshot.

"No problem," Billy said. "My walkie is a direct line to Operat—" He patted the empty spot on his leather belt. "Damn." Then searched around the catwalk. "Must've lost it during the bull ride."

"Okay, Kyra. Just stand by and let us know when a supe shows up. Over."

"*Ten-four. Over and out.*"

"Did you guys see those large rocks blow out of the hole?" Juan whispered.

Everyone nodded and gazed up into the darkness.

"Where did they go?" Stan asked.

"What goes up... must come down," said the disembodied voice of the sunburned raccoon lady.

Lidia gave a hissing intake of breath. "This isn't good."

"They probably blew apart," I said. "Ya know, vaporized or something from the pressure of the blast."

Billy shrugged. "Whatever the case, something would have hit us by now. We're good."

My attention returned to the construction site. The headlights of the vehicles and heavy equipment were much more dramatic in the hazy atmosphere, like stage lighting at a rock concert.

There was movement at the lip of the chasm.

Maybe it was a worker who'd fallen in after the blast.

More shadows danced along the interior of the crevasse.

Lightning flashed.

"Oh, geez!" Juan shouted. "Did you guys see that?"

"Yeah," I said. "Think it's a worker. Someone trying to climb out."

"No! *Up there*! In the clouds above us!"

EIGHT

WE STARED AT THE SWIRLING clouds overhead. Billy rose to his feet and aimed his flashlight skyward, but its beam failed to penetrate the gloom.

From somewhere high above, flapping wings broke the silence. Followed by an unholy screech.

We let out a collective gasp and the hair on my arms stood on end.

"What the hell?" Stan said. "What did you see up there?"

Juan kept his eyes to the sky and only shook his head.

Another screech—louder, closer—fell upon us.

"Oh, shit!" Stan said. "What the hell, man?"

Billy whipped his light back and forth, hoping to spot something.

"Turn it off," Lidia said.

I wanted to say, "No, wait!" That the light would help us see whatever was approaching. Then again, it could be attracted to the beam.

Obviously, Lidia wanted it off for that very reason.

"She's right, Billy," I said. "You should shut it off."

A shriek, somewhere to our right, was immediately answered by a guttural screech to our left. Then a snarl sounded opposite the pair.

It became terrifyingly clear that whatever had rocketed

out of that hole was much more dangerous than a bunch of falling rocks.

Stan whimpered and crouched beside the car. "Someone please tell me what the hell is up there!"

The heavens lit up in a spiderweb of lightning.

Within the flashing storm clouds, flying creatures circled the train like sharks in chum-filled water. The brief burst of light revealed their leathery wings—webbed, veiny, and spanning at least two dozen feet. Their bodies were thick and muscular. Their smooth, bald heads were crowned with large, pointed ears. Then the light extinguished, and the clouds went black.

Billy waved his flashlight around, apparently trying to track them.

"Turn that damn thing off!" Lidia repeated.

"Yeah. I think maybe you're ri—"

Something burst out of the darkness and blew past our heads. The wind from its massive wings rocked the train and knocked Billy back, slamming him so hard into the catwalk railing that his feet flew up and his body flipped over.

Through the walkway's steel mesh, we watched in horror as the screaming mechanic plunged nine stories to the ground, the flashlight in his hand illuminating his way.

"Oh, God!" Juan said.

Another pass of mighty wings and the car violently swayed again. Everyone screamed, but our noise was quickly overtaken by Billy's terrified cries, now growing louder.

He was *rising* back toward us.

A huge, bat-like creature—with Billy in its grasp—rocketed past the catwalk. As predator and prey soared for the storm clouds, the flashlight, aimed at the man's terrified face, revealed that the beast had a second set of arms that were coiled around the mechanic, pressing him into its massive, hairy chest.

A moment later, Billy was gone. Only the muted beam from his flashlight circled deep within the clouds, and his heart-wrenching cries echoed out of the darkness.

Suddenly, from various directions, a terrifying chorus of flapping wings and screeches filled the night.

The creatures zeroed in on their own, the one with the freshly caught prey.

The dot of light within the clouds violently jerked back and forth.

"Oh, God!" Billy screamed. "Oh, Jesus! Please! No! Help meeeee—"

His final word turned into a high-pitched squeal.

Then cut short.

The flashlight dropped out of the clouds, its beam spiraling in a freefall back to earth. It landed on the lift behind us and shattered.

Then the sky opened, raining blood and gore. Slimy, purple entrails splattered and draped over the railing like a sopping wet towel tossed on a clothesline. The mechanic's left leg, severed at the knee in fleshy petals of meat and gristle, bounced off the catwalk and fell to the ground over a hundred feet below.

"Oh, shit oh shit oh shit oh shit," Stan said. The deluge of horror flooding his brain reduced his vocabulary to the same two words.

Lightning flashed to reveal more shadows circling above.

"*Danny!*" Kyra's voice jumped out of the walkie-talkie. "*What the hell is happening up there?! We heard someone screaming. Over.*"

I sunk in my seat, pressed the walkie to my mouth, and whispered, "Send someone for help. Now! Get the cops. But do not come up. I repeat, do not come up. Things are flying around… trying to get us. They killed Billy."

"*What? You broke up after something about 'flying around.' What's going on? Who's hurt? Who was that screa—*"

A hellacious screech from above drowned out her words. I didn't know if she heard it way down in the station, but we sure as hell did up there.

"*Danny! Do you copy? Over.*"

"Shut that thing off!" Lidia said, barely above a whisper.

Considering how spot on she was about Billy and the flashlight, I blurted into the walkie, "Stay away. Do not come up. Send for help. Gotta go."

Before I could switch it off, Stan snatched it out of my hand and hurled the walkie-talkie over the edge.

"What the hell did you do that for?" I asked.

"You wouldn't shut up on that thing. You'll draw them to us."

Juan poked his face through the headrest. "That was stupid, man! Now we have no way of communicating with anybody below."

"But-but he wouldn't shut up."

"Our conversation was over. I was about to turn it off when you grabbed it."

"No, you weren't. Besides—"

"Okay! Enough!" Lidia snapped. "Everybody shut up!"

We sat in silence and stared up into the darkness.

After a long beat, Juan whispered to me, "Dude, we have to get out of here. Now. So, screw your stupid protocols about waiting for a supervisor. Those things already ate the big guy. We're next."

I nodded in agreement as fast as my heart was pounding, then searched for the key somewhere under my seat.

"Stan! Help me find the lap bar key."

Hugging the car's exterior, Stan shook his head and remained kneeling on the catwalk, trying to keep himself lower than everyone else in case of another aerial attack.

My fingernails painfully raked the steel floor. If I could get the key, I'd free myself and the couple behind me—and, if she could be reached, the raccoon lady—then have Stan escort them down the catwalk. As for the rest of the people already out on the track…?

I took a deep breath.

I'd have to climb over each seat, unload one person at a time, and escort them back to the catwalk while praying no one—including myself—slipped and fell to their death.

Brushing aside such a terrifying scenario, all that mattered was getting everyone to safety, so I could leave and find Stacy. I had to know she was okay. None of which could happen if I remained stuck in the freaking car.

Leaning over the lap bar, I continued my frantic search. My heart jackhammered in my ears, amplifying the sound of my heavy breathing.

"Wait," Juan said. "What's that noise?"

I gasped. Oh-no. Please, not again!

"It's coming from over there," Lidia said.

"Yeah. Look!"

I turned to find them staring at the construction site.

Then I heard it also… a faint chittering like the eerie sound made by cicadas, at first distant, but growing louder.

Loose dirt at the lip of the gorge vibrated and fell back into the earth. A dust cloud rose out of the chasm and hovered like a low hanging fog bank.

There was movement within the gloom.

A giant pair of segmented legs sprung out and planted on the edge of the fissure. The prickly limbs dug in deep and flexed.

Then a dark mass the size of a horse rose out of the haze.

NINE

GLIMPSED IN THE CONSTRUCTION vehicles' headlights, an enormous spider-like thing darted out of the hole and scurried into the shadows. As soon as it found shelter in the darkness, a wave of creatures erupted from the fissure.

If the flying things that killed Billy were scouts, then the cavalry had arrived.

There were bodies of all shapes and sizes. Some had exoskeletons, others coated in scales or leathery skin. They scuttled, slithered, and flew out of the crevasse. The more agile creatures scampered over the backs of the slower ones. They swarmed the construction equipment like fire ants defending their mound, scaling the vehicles, and climbing on top of each other until becoming three or four layers deep.

Within the headlight beams were flashes of mandibles, fangs, stingers, pincers, claws, and beady black eyes. Then the lights shattered, plunging the work area into darkness.

Lightning strobed, revealing the infestation spreading across the ground. A rolling army of insectoid, reptilian, and arachnid invaders headed directly for the river of light that was the gridlocked highway. Once past the interstate, they would hit the park itself, with Shock Waves being the first ride in their path.

The cars in the right-hand lane of the westbound stretch were overtaken first. It was then that the screams of terror reached their crescendo.

A black crab the size of a rhino grabbed a sedan in its bulbous pincers, hoisting the car into the air and flipping it onto its side.

The driver, a man in his late twenties, fled from the beast outside his window by scrambling up and over the woman still belted in the vehicle's passenger seat. While she slapped him and begged for help, the coward used her as a step stool to climb through the passenger window.

Just as he made it out, a pincer sheared off the driver's door and thrust itself inside. Seconds later, the woman's screams abruptly stopped, and a torrent of blood erupted out the passenger window.

With the car still hovering on its side, the man fought to maintain his balance while slipping and sliding in the woman's blood.

Before he could make it to the bumper and jump, his chest exploded in a pink mist.

He stumbled from the impact and looked down. A barbed tentacle, stretching from out of the darkness, pierced his sternum. His eyes fluttered and limbs twitched. Warm blood seeped down his belly. His bladder released.

Then the tentacle pulled taut and ripped him off his feet, reeling him into the shadows to be consumed by whatever waited on the other end.

A swirling mass of tick-like things the size of rats enveloped a pickup truck. The tires hissed, then exploded, dropping the vehicle to its rims. A window shattered, and the monstrosities poured into the cab.

The driver bolted from the truck. Only a few steps into his escape, he was swarmed by the miniature army.

They rushed up his legs and burrowed into his skin.

His flesh bubbled and stretched. He convulsed, his spine stiffened, and when he let off an unholy howl, the creatures flooded his mouth, ramming their way down his throat.

Moments later, they reappeared, exploding from his skull, chest, and stomach in an obscene spray of brains, blood, and intestines. His knees unhinged, dropping his soiled, lifeless body to the ground, where it continued being devoured from the inside out.

Sitting on an idling motorcycle in the middle of the highway, a young man gawked at the horrors around him.

A translucent blob, some sort of earthbound jellyfish, slid out from behind a car and rushed him.

When his fight-or-flight instinct finally kicked in, the man revved the throttle and shot forward to escape the creature, weaving between two vehicles already under attack. He narrowly dodged snapping pincers to his left and the swipe of sharp talons to his right.

As the bike sped up, he glanced over his shoulder and saw the blob giving chase.

He gunned the motorcycle, threw another look back, and caught his pursuer now in midair, leaping over him.

The creature landed a few yards ahead of the rider. Its oblong body flipped up and popped open. Fleshy folds snapped back, throwing out ribbons of slime and unsheathing dual rows of spindly legs that stretched wide.

Before the motorcyclist could release the throttle, he drove straight into the wall of flesh. Like a Venus Flytrap, it snapped shut, completely engulfing man and machine. The slick, pulsating tissue squeezed tight, vacuum-sealing itself over its prey. The man opened his mouth as if to scream but only inhaled the suffocating membrane. Then bone and metal crunched, and the semi-transparent outline of the struggling rider popped, leaving a large, crimson blossom beneath the tissue.

From out of the darkness, a gigantic tentacle dragged an upside-down Volkswagen Beetle across the highway in a shower of sparks... which ignited the leaking gas tank of a Cadillac turned on its side. The explosion took out a few nearby creatures, but their numbers were quickly replenished by a fresh surge rising to the surface.

Gigantic pincers, incisors, and claws became industrial can openers, tearing into vehicles to reach their warm, juicy, screaming contents.

As the onslaught continued, and the pickings grew slim, those unable to find food expanded their search beyond the highway.

They scrambled over their brethren and made a beeline for the chain-link fence enclosing The Lone Star Land Amusement Park.

TEN

THE GROUND HAD LEGS and moved. Thousands of limbs clicked, clacked, and scratched. The nerve-shredding sounds prickled my scalp. Their musky scent, an acrid stench like ammonia and rotting fish, rode the wind. Illuminated by lightning flashes and the burning wreckage strewn across the highway, the creatures plowed through the chain-link fence alongside our ride.

The horde advanced as a living wave, ready to crash into the station house containing my crew. My friends.

"No-no-no-no-no-no-no," I whispered.

Then ear-piercing screams exploded out of the station.

The creatures on the front line smashed into the building, scurrying up the exit ramp and over the railings. As they pushed their way through the rear of the structure, guests scrambled out its front, fleeing the slaughter happening within.

Those who escaped didn't get very far when dark shadows along the roof sprang into action with a loud buzzing sound. Lightning flashed, revealing jet-black giant wasps with huge pickaxe forelegs. They landed on their prey, jackhammering into flesh and muscle, splintering bone, and drenching the area in arterial spray.

A woman was impaled through each shoulder by two wasps. Like a strip of Velcro, she was ripped in half in a geyser of blood. The pieces flew off in separate directions, leaving only a steaming pile of entrails on the ground where she once stood.

A man (wearing a white t-shirt with the faded words 'Frankie Say Relax') was cornered by a giant wasp. The thing went airborne and punched its stinger into his chest. The flesh swelled so much from the venom, the pores of his skin opened and honeycombed. Then it popped in an explosion of pus and blood. The man fell limp, and the creature engulfed him. It chomped on his skull, cracking it open and removing everything above the eye sockets in two bites.

Once the screaming stopped and the feast began, those without a meal continued forward, moving deeper into the park.

The next ride in their path was The Rip-Roaring Rapids.

"Help me find the fucking key!" I screamed at Stan while wrenching on the lap bar. I had to get out of there, had to reach Stacy.

Stan remained crouching on the grated walkway, cowering beside the train, babbling incoherently.

"Dude!" Juan yelled at him. "Move your ass and help him find the key!"

Receiving no response, Juan threw his ball cap at the young man, hoping to snap him out of his paralysis (or, at the very least, piss him off enough so they'd lock eyes.)

The hat bounced off Stan's chest and landed on the catwalk.

"Oh… your hat…" Stan said, blankly staring down at the ball cap.

With Stan now utterly useless, Juan and Lidia helped me search for the key, leaning forward as far as their lap bar allowed. While I raked the floorboard, they felt around the seat cushion.

A gust of wind hit Juan's ball cap, sliding it sideways until it teetered on the edge of the catwalk. Stan crawled to the hat and snatched it up before it fell.

Obviously, his priorities lay elsewhere.

Still on all fours, he exhaled and stared through the metal grating. He suddenly shrieked in terror and, while clutching the ball cap to his chest, climbed to his feet and hopped across the catwalk as if performing a fire walk.

Screaming hysterically, he leaped into the car in front of me, stood on the seat, and pointed down.

"There's something there! Right below us! Under the train!"

A flap of mighty wings. A gust of wind. A deafening screech from above. Then Stan was ripped up into the darkness.

We screamed and ducked for cover.

I felt the key lying on the floor, grabbed it, and clutched it two-fisted to my heart, paranoid I might drop it.

"I got it. I got it!" I slid across the seat toward the catwalk and felt for the keyhole outside the car.

Something clamped over my shoulder, pinning me in place.

I yelped.

My head and one arm hung out of the car.

"Don't. Move," Juan whispered through the headrest. "Something's here. Look down." He slowly released his grip.

I saw a long, segmented body with dozens of legs hooked on the underside of the catwalk. It rhythmically crept upside down toward the front of the train. Its wiry body hair scraped the metal and poked through the grating.

Hanging halfway out of the car, I held my breath, terrified the thing would feel my exhale across its belly.

Creeping to the end of the catwalk, it seemed attracted

to the commotion of the passengers yelling for help.

A leg telescoped and hooked on top of the walkway. Then another leg rose. And another. Dozens more followed before it gracefully twisted and pulled itself upright.

The thing looked like a gigantic centipede coated in needles of hair. It sat waiting, cloaked in the shadows, aimed at the front of the train.

The shouts for help continued. With all the mayhem and carnage taking place, it was insane how these people kept drawing attention to themselves.

I wanted to scream at them to shut up but doing so might draw the creature back to us.

The monstrous centipede climbed into the empty seat behind the lady with the raccoon sunburn.

Another centipede appeared, crawling up from under the train. Then another. The creatures entwined and became a writhing mass of legs.

The sunburned lady must have felt them breathing down her neck. She turned, went wide-eyed, and a bone-chilling scream erupted from her mouth.

ELEVEN

STRIKING LIKE VENOMOUS SNAKES, the creatures attacked the raccoon lady and other guests up front.

During the onslaught, I sank in my seat and heard the morbid symphony of screams, tearing flesh, cracking bones, and the dying gasps of my fellow passengers. A warm, coppery spray spritzed me, and something thumped with a wet splat against the empty seat ahead.

I jumped and covered my ears to drown out the loud chewing and slurping sounds.

My body trembled so hard I thought I was having a seizure. Then I realized I was being shaken by Juan and slapped by Lidia.

"Get up!" "Get us out of here!" "Now!"

Ashamed of my moment of weakness, I wiped away the snot and tears, then took an assertive breath and resumed searching for the tiny keyhole alongside the car.

Juan patted my shoulder.

"Atta boy, hoss. Just get us outta here. You focus on that, and I'll cover our asses."

He held up his gigantic western belt buckle, which could be slung around by its leather belt and slammed into an attacker's face almost like a medieval mace and chain. Pretty solid for a makeshift weapon.

As the feeding sounds grew louder, I ran a hand across the outside of the car until a finger dipped into the keyhole.

I jabbed the key in.

A screech echoed from somewhere above.

Terrified, I sucked in a breath between gritted teeth, and frantically jiggled the key until the lock clicked.

"Look out!" Juan pushed me down in my seat.

Something flew over us, rippling our hair and clothes with its wings. The bat creature landed somewhere at the front of the train, out of sight, where the centipedes were feasting. There were throaty growls, hissing, and chittering, then heavy thumps and thuds against the train's fiberglass body. A struggle took place between the two species, most likely over food.

Another bat swooped down to join its winged companion in battle.

While the pandemonium continued up front, I used it to our advantage and made my move. I pushed my lap bar up. Remaining low, I climbed out of the car and onto the catwalk.

Crouching, I unlocked Juan and Lidia's lap bar and waved the couple out.

Lightning flashed overhead, then raindrops fell.

The storm had finally arrived.

The couple motioned to ask if I was ready to head downhill.

I shrugged and half-heartedly hitched a thumb over my shoulder toward the front of the train. The lump in my throat blocked any words from coming out, but they knew what I was inferring... we had to at least check to see if anyone was still alive.

Lidia shook her head and pulled her husband's arm.

"No. We'll find help. That's all we can do."

Juan leaned closer. "She's right." He held up his belt. "We can't fight them with just this. We gotta get help. Real help."

The noise from all the tearing and chewing—along with the occasional splintering of bone—told me it was already too late. No one was screaming anymore. It was impossible for anyone to survive, especially with a lap bar locking their ass in place.

Venturing closer, even for a quick peek, would be suicidal.

"*Help... me...*" A plea came from over the hill, somewhere at the front of the train.

We whirled toward it.

"*... help...*"

The voice was so faint and racked with pain that it made it impossible to determine whether it was male or female, adult or child.

I looked back at Juan and Lidia. Knowing what needed to be done, I closed my eyes, exhaled, and lowered my head, trying to work up the courage to act.

When I opened my eyes, the couple had slunk away and were about to head downhill.

My shoulders slumped.

Juan mouthed an apology before continuing down.

"*... help me...*"

My chest tightened, and I shook uncontrollably (and it had nothing to do with the heavy rain falling in thick sheets.) After a deep breath, I began slowly crawling toward the voice at the end of the catwalk.

Inch by agonizing inch, I moved closer, wondering if I was crawling to my death.

I'd never see Stacy again. Never be able to say I was sorry or goodbye, or hear her say, 'I love you' one last time while holding her tight.

The blinding rain pounded my back.

Peering down through the grating, I heard a loud thud and felt the catwalk buckle.

I looked up, and a shadowy figure with glowing eyes crouched in front of me.

TWELVE

THE MONSTROSITY STARING ME down was neither a centipede nor a bat. It was about four feet tall, had a coiled shell for a body, spindly legs, and sharp pincers resembling needle-nose pliers. Incandescent orbs peeked out from under its cracked shell, which had a milky sack bulging out of it.

The thing was like a hermit crab from hell, one that was ready to burst from its casing.

I had no idea where it came from. Maybe it climbed up a support beam or out of the first loop. It really didn't matter. What did was its aggressive stance, which warned me an attack was imminent.

I backpedaled, slipped, and fell flat on my ass with my legs spread wide.

The thing lunged forward, its snapping pincers homing in on, of all things, my nuts.

A flash of silver and gold *whooshed* over my head, then the creature violently rocked sideways and stumbled.

Before it could regain its footing, a second blow to the body popped its bulging sack. An explosion of thick custard splattered the train and dripped through the grating.

Juan stood over me, swinging that big-ass belt buckle of his like a lasso.

He pummeled the screeching beast with it again and

again, beating it until the thing teetered on the edge of the catwalk just below the railing. The final blow knocked the ugly bastard off, punching its one-way ticket on a nine-story drop.

Lidia and Juan hoisted me to my feet.

"C'mon," Lidia said. "Everyone's dead."

"So, move your ass," Juan added, "before we leave you for good this time!"

I thanked the couple and maneuvered past them.

The rain pelted down. While it provided good cover, we couldn't see more than a few feet in front of us. Given the slick conditions and steep decline, we descended slowly.

My hand slid along the cold metal railing and into something spongy and tepid. A glistening strip of muscle hung there, dribbling rainwater off both flaccid ends. I quickly wiped my hand on my shorts and pressed on.

My mind raced with white-hot intensity.

I had to get ahold of a weapon, something to use to protect myself when setting out for Stacy.

If she was in danger, there was no way I could just sit at my ride and wait for help. I had to find her. I owed her that much, still feeling sick about how I left things earlier in the canteen. All because I asked her to consider a procedure that could fix our "problem." After I pleaded my case, she informed me, with tears in her eyes, she'd be keeping the baby and it was up to me if I was going to be man enough to stick around and help raise it. To be a father.

Her words stung because she knew my dad ran out on my family when I was six, and how I never forgave him for it. Although she used that against me, I couldn't blame her for doing so.

I deserved worse.

I just hoped it wasn't waiting for me somewhere below, in the darkness.

THIRTEEN

WHOEVER SHE WAS, SHE was hot as hell. I started a conversation with her while waiting in line at the park's job orientation.

Afterwards, Stacy and I continued our chat in the employee parking lot when a gold Camaro, blaring Kiss's "Love Gun," zoomed up to us.

Its driver, a dude named Beef, who had gelled spiky hair like a porcupine, asked if we were both new hires.

We nodded.

"Wicked!" he said and handed us a flyer on neon paper. "Feel free to spread the word to any hot babes. The more, the merrier. See you guys there."

After revving the engine, Beef and his Love Gun zipped away to the next group exiting orientation.

We examined the Xerox copy of his handwritten flyer that announced *Beef's Big Kegger*.

BYOB:
Bring Your Own Beer!
Bring Your Own Bimbo!
Bring Your Own Boy Toy!
Bring Your Own Birth Control!

A disclaimer said that The Lone Star Land Amusement

Park had nothing to do with the jam. It also had his address and a hand-drawn map with directions from the park to his house.

So, we thought, "What the hell?" and our first date was a kegger thrown by a seventeen-year-old ride foreman whose parents were out of town.

Although it was a chance to mingle and make tons of friends at our new job, Stacy and I pretty much kept to ourselves.

First, we hung out in the kitchen while the traffic was light, then on the back patio when things got too crowded.

When the party spilled out back, we headed to the front to talk on the hood of my car.

I pulled out a jambox from the backseat of my Buick and dug through a case of mix tapes, eventually selecting one with an assortment of new wave, rock, and, more importantly, power ballads.

The stars were out bright, so we laid back on the hood, shoulder to shoulder, gazing up at the sky while chatting about our favorite movies, music, and childhood memories.

She slid a little closer, then I did the same.

Her touch was comforting, her hair smelled like coconut, either from her hairspray or shampoo.

I knew what song was coming up on the tape and planned to make my move by leaning over and kissing her.

I was nervous as hell.

After what seemed like the longest minute of my life waiting for Van Halen's "Why Can't This Be Love" to finish, Depeche Mode's "Stripped" started rolling.

Right as the chorus kicked in, I took a deep breath and...

She leaned over and kissed me. (Later, she told me I was taking too long and that she wanted to kiss me a few songs earlier.)

As the song played, she climbed on top, and we continued kissing. Her long, crunchy, teased out hair cascaded onto my face, tickling it. I reached up and held it back by gently cradling her face the way I'd seen it done in movies.

While we made out, a group of guys strolling up to the party yelled, "Get a room!" We ignored them and continued kissing, rolling around on the hood.

When the party broke up at dawn and people stumbled to their cars, we were all puckered out from our make-out session. Kicked back against my windshield, she held my hand while I had my free arm wrapped around her.

We watched the sun rise, then drove to the amusement park to start our first day of work.

I thought about her all day long and couldn't wait to see her when we got off.

When our shift finally ended, we met up at wardrobe to change out of our park-issued uniforms, then headed to the mall so she could pick up the Depeche Mode album with "Stripped" on it. I guess that officially meant it was 'our song.'

After the record store, we saw a movie at the mall's complex and had a late dinner at Whataburger.

All this while going on over thirty-six hours without sleep.

Crawling into bed that night, I already missed her and couldn't wait to see her again in the morning.

More importantly, I knew, then and there, I wanted to spend the rest of my life with this girl.

And that I would do anything for her.

FOURTEEN

NEARING THE BOTTOM OF the hill, I thought of what could be used as a weapon. A broomstick or squeegee handle could be snapped off and turned into a spear. Or broken in two to make a pair of batons.

No, a spear was better for maintaining a safer distance from any threat.

Once we reached level track, I climbed down into the sopping wet grass and helped Lidia and Juan to the ground.

The murky station loomed over us.

"Okay," I said, motioning to the building. "You guys ready?"

"Bullshit," Juan said, barely above a whisper. "We're not going in there. It could still be crawling with 'em."

"The only way out of here is up. And inside are stairs leading up to the dock."

Juan gave it another look. "Nuh-uh. No way."

"Listen. The entire track is enclosed by a nine-foot fence topped with barbed wire."

"Maybe," Lidia said. "But not there." She pointed to the large breach in the fence made by the stampeding horde.

I shook my head. "You crazy? That's where they came from."

Juan studied the opening.

"Don't do it," I said. "That hole at the construction site?

It could have another wave of those things making their way to the surface."

"And what about the ones already in the park? They could be out there waiting for us."

"Or they could've moved on. Maybe heading for downtown or nearby neighborhoods."

Panic suddenly washed over Lidia's face. "Oh, no."

Juan grabbed her hand. "Hey, babe. They're fine. Nothing happened to them. Trust m—"

A deafening roar came from the highway.

As we scrambled for cover under the coaster's elevated track, an upside-down car slid past the fence's opening in a shower of sparks.

I turned to the couple with an *'I told ya so'* expression.

They exchanged a glance, then Lydia said, "Okay. I guess you know your way around here, huh?"

"Can you get us to the overflow parking lot?" Juan asked.

"Yeah. Why?"

Both remained silent.

"What? Is that where you're parked? Please tell me you're not concerned about your car at a time like this."

"Screw you, man," Juan said. "We walked here. And screw you for implying that I only care about my c—"

Lidia squeezed her husband's hand.

Juan exhaled and stared at his feet for a moment.

"Look," he said. "At the back of overflow parking, there's a heavily wooded lot with a few picnic tables up front."

I knew the spot. It was the only place to park for the night shift on busy weekends. It sucked because it was a twenty-minute walk to wardrobe.

"At the back of that lot is a brick wall that separates the park property from a residential neighborhood. Mi abuela lives—"

"His grandmother," Lidia said.

Juan rolled his eyes. "Yeah, my *grandmother*."

"Don't get all pissy. I'm just telling him in case he doesn't know what abuela means."

"I'm not pissy."

"Ah, yeah. You kinda are."

"I am not!"

"You are, dude," I said. "And I didn't know what abuela means, but I do now." I winked at Lidia.

She smiled and backhanded Juan's arm. "See?"

"Oh, my God," he said. "Can I continue?"

Lidia nodded.

"Thank you. Sooo… Abuelita lives in the neighborhood behind that wooded lot. She's watching our little boy while we're having a date night. He's too small to ride anything because of your dumb height restrictions, so she agreed to watch him while we're out here."

I shook my head, waiting for them to get to the point.

Lidia jumped in. "Like you said, if those things are moving across the park, it's only a matter of time before they make it to nearby neighborhoods, if they haven't already."

She gently grabbed my arm. "Please. We have to get back to our baby. You know the way around the park better than anybody, especially all the shortcuts. With you leading the way, we can reach him much faster than if we tried to do it on our own. Especially during a flippin' blackout."

Juan held up a wad of cash. "We'll pay you to take us there. I got fifty-three bucks here."

I began mapping out the best route in my head.

More importantly, I thought about strength in numbers.

"Please," Lidia said. "We have to get to our baby. To make sure he and Abuelita are okay."

I waved off their money.

"I'll take you. No charge. But we'll have to make a slight detour and get my girlfriend along the way. She works at Rapids, and I'm not leaving without her. We get Stacy, then I'll get you to your boy. Deal?"

Lidia nodded. Juan and I shook on it.

We faced the dark station.

"Okay," I said. "Now, we need to find some weapons."

FIFTEEN

TORRENTIAL RAINFALL DIMMED THE burning wreckage along the highway. In muted firelight, the Shock Waves' station resembled a decrepit haunted house sitting on the edge of a void.

Ironically, in order to get out, we had to enter.

I took the lead. I traveled the route so many times I could've done it blindfolded, which wasn't far from our current situation.

Like touring a Halloween haunted house, we walked single file through the darkness. Lidia held the back of my shirt. Juan clutched her shoulder from the rear.

Once we were a few feet under the dock and out of the rain, I paused to let my eyes adjust. Visibility was limited, so I felt my way around.

Water leaked through the floorboards from the level above, soaking us. The station's roof must have sustained damage during the attack. If my calculations were right, we were under the loading dock, where the guests waited in line at the stalls. Which meant the stairs should be right around the corner.

Rainwater dripped down my face and over my lips. I tasted something coppery. My stomach instantly soured, remembering how, as a kid, I was prone to nosebleeds, and it was that same salty, metallic taste.

Lightning strobed for a few seconds, allowing a glimpse of my hands and the front of my uniform.

Everything was maroon.

Behind me, Lidia gasped and let go of my shirt.

I spun around and saw that she and Juan were also painted red.

Our eyes darted up, and before the lightning burst ended, we saw nothing but blood dripping from the ceiling.

Repulsed and horrified, we frantically wiped our faces, spat, and carelessly raced through the darkness to get out from under the gore.

We found the stairs and rushed up.

Hitting the top landing, we entered the back area of the dock and got slammed by the stench of a slaughterhouse—a toxic mixture of feces, entrails, and copper.

Reluctantly, we moved forward.

The broom closet lay ahead. Beyond it, an open doorway leading into the station house where the guests waited in line. Considering all the blood that had been dripping on us, I didn't want to go any farther, didn't want to see what was around that corner.

Lidia gently nudged me to keep moving. I hadn't realized I'd stopped.

"You see something?" Juan whispered.

I shook my head.

"Then get your ass in gear." He motioned to the stairwell we climbed out of. "I think something's following us. I heard a noise down there."

I pried loose a splintered board from the damaged wall to use as a temporary weapon. Lidia did the same.

I reached for the doorknob to the closet.

A thud came from our rear. We jumped and raised our weapons.

An enormous pile of rubble from a partially collapsed

wall sat ahead. Before it could be written off as only settling debris, something moved within its shadows.

We retreated a few steps and stopped when someone rose from behind the mound.

"Danny?"

It was Kyra. She pointed a broomstick at us like a spear.

"Holy crap!" I said, leaving the shadows and crossing into the firelight from the burning highway. "Are you okay?"

She eyed me up and down and stepped back. "Are *you*?"

It took a moment to realize the reason for her hesitation. She was staring at three people drenched in blood.

"Yeah. It—it's not mine. I'm okay. We're okay."

She nodded but kept her distance. Something in her hand glinted in the firelight.

It was a pair of glasses. Deb's glasses. One of the thick lenses was cracked.

Kyra held them up. "I found them. They had blood on them." Her voice trembled. "But I cleaned them off, so she doesn't freak out when I give them back to her."

"Where is she? And where's Greg?"

She shrugged, nervously giggled, and returned to the glasses. "Deb's gonna be so pissed that they're cracked. Ya know? I betcha she blames me for it."

Obviously, Kyra was still in shock. I refused to say anything that might quash her false optimism. After all, I wouldn't want someone doing it to me.

I stuck my head under the rainwater pouring in from the damaged roof to wash off all the blood. While scrubbing clean, I noticed the exit ramp was demolished, reduced to a deadfall of lumber. Guess we'd be leaving through the ride's entrance.

"So, what about the supply closet?" Juan said, reaching for the knob. "Anything in it we can use for a—?"

"Wait!" Kyra said, rushing forward.

But Juan had already opened the door.

A collective gasp and muffled screams flooded out.

We stared in.

Within the cramped, murky space, people were packed two layers deep against the far wall. One of the occupants shoved a broomstick in our face.

Kyra rushed forward to calm everyone.

The group dispersed the best they could within the small area, most breaking off into pairs. But no one stepped outside. The closet must have given them a false sense of security. Although its four walls ran about ten feet high, there was no ceiling. It was like an extra tall bathroom stall, but one without the open gaps at the bottom. If another attack were to occur, anything could drop in from the rafters or crawl over the walls.

"They all guests?" I asked.

"Yeah," Kyra said. "I tried to help more, but everyone just… just…" She lowered her head.

"Hey," I said. "You did good."

Kyra exhaled.

"No, honey," Lidia said. "He's right. Not only did you save these people, but you were out here protecting them. Anybody else would be hiding in there, right alongside them."

Kyra scoffed. "I'm claustrophobic. I tried to stay in there, but totally freaked. I'm only out here because it's the lesser of two evils." She scanned the shadows. "Or so I think."

"Whatever the case, you're kick-ass in my book," Juan said.

Lidia gently squeezed Kyra's shoulder. "Yep. Mine too, sweety."

While Juan and Lidia washed up under the flowing rainwater, I returned to the closet's occupants. Quick introductions were made since we didn't have time for much more.

Harry and Patty were an old married couple, at least in their fifties. They were decked out in red t-shirts and hats plastered with The Lone Star Land's gaudy logo. Typical tourists, here for the various attractions our city had to offer. Yesterday, they'd toured the armory for the Texas Army National Guard. Today, lucky them, they came to the park. They said something about being from up north, but I already started tuning them out.

Anna, a young woman holding her year-old baby, Ryan, was doing a damn good job of keeping the kid quiet. As tears rolled down her cheeks, she recalled waiting at the exit ramp for her boyfriend (Ryan's father) to get off the ride when all hell broke loose. She never saw what happened to him but was grateful that Kyra ushered her and the toddler into the shelter. I glanced at Ryan and couldn't help but think of mine and Stacy's predicament, the one before the lights went out. I gently caressed Ryan's head and, not having much experience with babies, kind of wound up petting him. Anna gave me a quizzical look as if to say, "You know he's not a dog, right?"

I pulled back, cleared my throat, and moved on to the two love birds, Mike and Vickie—both around my age. Looking like they just stepped out of a J.Crew catalogue, they clung to each other, although he seemed to be the one doing most of the clinging. Mike asked if I was going to get them out of there. I told them I was about to head out and they were welcome to join me if they wanted.

The final occupant, Todd, was a thirteen-year-old, short, skinny white kid with a curly, sandy-blonde mullet. He wore an Iron Maiden t-shirt with Eddie, the band's mascot, plastered across the front. Todd was the one aiming the spear at us earlier. Only stating his name and that his mom dropped him off alone at the park for the day, he was a dude of few words.

Our newly acquired baggage wasn't good. We needed to move fast, reach Stacy, and, as promised, get Juan and Lidia to their kid. Now I was responsible for a group of guests. Although not giving a rat's ass about my job at the moment, I was still in uniform, and these people were looking at me for help. I couldn't abandon them.

Strength in numbers, right?

But when it included an old couple and a baby, that theory kind of went limp.

Juan approached me. "Clock is ticking, sport. Where's the phone? If the line is back up, we should call for help before heading out."

He was right. Enough with the pleasantries.

"Okay. Follow me."

SIXTEEN

UNFORTUNATELY, SINCE RIDE PHONES were interior lines, we wouldn't be able to dial out for the police. But if we could get ahold of someone at operations, security, or some other department, they could send for help. After that, I would immediately call Rapids to try to reach Stacy.

Separating from the group, Juan and I peeked around the corner and into the station.

The dock was empty except for a few abandoned items: purses, a fanny pack, a cowboy hat, stuffed animal prizes, and (oddly enough) an untouched platter of ultimate nachos that balanced on a wood railing. There were also glistening piles of guts, chunks of meat, clumps of hair, and blood everywhere.

And, my God, the smell. We continued staring at what had been dripping on us earlier while under the dock, and I wanted to throw up all over again.

Juan and I cautiously approached the control booth. A large hole was punched through the front of it. Claw marks scarred the wood paneling. Although the phone's receiver was still attached to the wall, the handset was off its cradle, its cord stretched taut and disappearing through the hole.

I grabbed the cord and reeled it in. The phone—with someone's hand still attached—shot up and smacked me in the chest.

I gasped and shuffled away from the bloody appendage.

The hand was severed mid-forearm and had red ribbons of meat dangling from the end like it had been bitten or torn off.

Even worse was the wide, leather watchband buckled around its wrist like a shackle.

"Oh, shit... Greg..." My knees felt rubbery.

Juan snatched up the hand clutching the phone. He sucked in a breath as if about to dive into an icy pool, then pried the fingers loose. Each digit snapped like a twig. Once Greg's severed hand fell and hit the floor with a dull thud, Juan put the phone to his ear and pressed the receiver a few times.

"I'm not hearing anything."

I tried it myself. Although it was an internal line, there should've been a dial tone.

"It's dead."

Juan took the phone and tossed it aside.

"Enough bullshit. If we wanna make it out of here, we need better weapons."

We returned to the group to rummage through the closet, but Lidia and Kyra had already beat us to it. They handed us two makeshift spears: wooden handles from a push broom and a floor squeegee, each snapped off at one end, leaving a jagged tip.

"Think it'll do some damage?" Lidia said.

Juan sized up the weapon. "You can bet your sweet bippy it will."

He re-threaded his belt through his Wranglers and knocked twice on the huge western buckle with a gold silhouette of a man riding a bucking bull.

"1985. Fort Worth Stockyards. Took home the gold that night."

Giddy with pride, Lidia gave her husband a short round of applause, clapping lightly in front of her face.

"Yay, babe!" she said. "Y'all should've seen him that night. He was *so* awesome!"

Being a kindred spirit to sporting competitions, Kyra smiled. "Nice. Congratulations."

"Thanks, ladies." Juan turned to me. "So, what's the plan, chief?"

"I need to find Stacy."

Juan and Lidia looked confused.

"Stacy. My girlfriend. Remember?! The one we're taking the slight detour for."

"Oooh."

"Once we get her, I'll get you guys out of the park and back to your kid."

They smiled. That's all they wanted to hear.

Kyra motioned to the closet full of people. "What about them?"

Todd, the young headbanger, was the only one standing outside the open door, leaning on his spear, listening to our conversation.

"Honestly, I think everyone should come with us. That closet isn't really safe. It—"

A faint groan came from the other side of the station.

A chill snaked up my spine.

We stared wide-eyed at each other for a beat, then spun to the sound.

The flickering firelight from the highway caused the shadows to dance and come alive.

I warily inched forward for a better view, keeping my distance from the deep, murky trough dividing the station.

Another groan. Louder. Racked with pain.

My eyes darted to the building's entrance. A set of stairs

went down to a turnstile. Past it was a fenced-in, zig-zagging walkway that led to the entrance of the ride.

"It's coming from the bottom of the steps," I said. "I think someone's down there. By the turnstile."

"Are we sure it's a person?" Juan said. "It was only a moan. Might be one of those things."

"*Help...*" a weak voice called out.

"Welp," Juan said. "Guess that answers that."

Todd came up beside Lidia and Kyra. Everyone else peeked out of the closet like gophers ready to dart back into their holes.

"Juan and I will check it out. You guys stay here and," I nodded at the guests, "protect them."

"Be careful," Lidia and Kyra said in unison.

I looked at Juan and motioned to the trough. "We'll have to jump it. You cool with that?"

"Yep."

"I'll go first."

I backpedaled enough to get a running start, then bolted forward. The width of the trough was roughly five feet, which I knew I could easily clear. Yet, in midair, I made the mistake of glancing down into the black void while recalling the iconic *Jaws* poster. Thinking about it made me shiver, and my balls pulled up and in like a frightened turtle.

I landed on the other side and my foot slipped on something wet and squishy, like a mound of spaghetti. Quickly regaining my balance, I refused to look back at what I'd stepped in. I had a good idea what it was and didn't need confirmation, otherwise, I'd probably barf and lose my nerve to continue.

Juan avoided the entrails and landed much more gracefully.

We raised our spears and crept toward the entrance.

By now, the rain had slowed to a fine mist.

"There!" Juan said in a hushed tone.

He pointed past the turnstile to a woman lying on the walkway at the bottom of the steps.

She was only visible from the chest up, the rest of her hidden around the corner of the wood plank fence. She had one arm outstretched, trying to pull herself forward around the bend.

At first, I didn't recognize her because of the mask of pain twisting her face. That, and the fact she wasn't wearing her thick coke-bottle glasses.

"Deb!"

I ran down the steps, taking two at a time, and hopped the turnstile.

Juan was more cautious with his approach.

With her eyes bulging and face beet red, Deb reached out for me.

"Danny…?" Her voice was weak. Strained. "Please… help…"

Stopping just shy of the corner, I knelt and took her hand. "It's gonna be okay."

But then I leaned forward, and my eyes shot wide open when I saw what was waiting around the turn.

SEVENTEEN

SOMETHING HAD DEB IN its mouth. Everything below her waist was completely engulfed by its maw, including her other arm tightly pinned to her side.

The thing was reptilian, a giant lizard with sandpapery flesh. The way it was devouring her whole, while still alive, reminded me of a nature show where a python slowly swallowed an entire calf. Like the snake on the show, the lizard's jaw was stretched obscenely wide, so much so that within the limited confines of the fenced walkway, its bulbous head obscured its body.

I had no idea if it had legs… was a snake… or a giant head that rolled there like a demonic Pac-Man.

Its large, black, emotionless eyes glared ahead before slowly rolling back in their sockets as if going into some food-induced coma. Its jaw loudly cracked and unhinged wider, drawing Deb in deeper.

She hissed through gritted teeth and slid in a few inches more. Her eyes ballooned like they were ready to pop. A large vein bulged across her purple forehead.

The young woman's lower body was being squeezed like a tube of toothpaste, the pressure building so much in her upper half that it would soon rupture its contents.

We had to act fast. I didn't know the condition of her lower half, if it was slowly being dissolved by the creature's stomach acid or if anything at all was left intact. Given that Deb was conscious and speaking, there was still hope we could do something for her, no matter how risky.

"Deb, listen to me." I grabbed her wrist and forearm. "I'm gonna pull you out."

"What?!" Juan said. He bent down and hovered over my shoulder. "Are you crazy?"

"I know this girl. I'm not leaving her like this."

"Dude, you ever see someone try to take a bone away from a stray dog? You're gonna royally piss this thing off."

"You just poke it in the eye, and I'll pull her out when it recoils."

"Just poke it in the eye?! What the hell? What are we? The Three Stooges?"

"C'mon, man! Use your spear. You don't have to get any closer. Just lean over me and stab it."

"If it doesn't let her go, you could tear the poor girl in half."

"It'll work. Just go for the eye on three. One…"

"Shit!" Juan aimed his spear at the thing.

"Two…"

I tightened my grip on Deb's arm.

"Three!"

Juan went for the eye, but his spear came up short and only tapped its cheek.

I yanked back, and Deb slipped right out of my grasp. It must have been the combo of the rain, our sweat, her blood, and the creature's saliva that made her skin so slick.

Thrown off balance, I fell on my ass and took out Juan at the knees. He flew up and over my shoulder.

I slammed against the wood fence. Juan landed on the ground in front of me with a heavy thud.

Although we made the same amount of racket, the creature's eyes clicked down and locked only on Juan.

With (a still conscious) Deb dangling out of its mouth, the thing growled and reared up on two legs.

"Oh, ffffuu...," I whispered.

The huge reptile lunged forward.

I grabbed Juan and pulled him up the stairs.

"Run-buddy-run!"

Giving chase in bipedal locomotion, the thing pushed aside the turnstile and waddled up the steps after us. Webbed feet with large talons slapped and scratched the wooden stairs. A groaning Deb flopped around wildly in its mouth.

We hit the top landing and a clawed foot swiped Juan's legs out from under him, knocking him to the station's floor.

I didn't know if the beast was attacking to defend its catch, was hungry for more food, or was too stupid to realize it already had a mouth full of it.

Whatever the case, it rushed Juan.

I speared the thing in the side, knocking it off course.

The creature let off a muffled scream and whirled around, slamming Deb's upper body into mine. It was like being clobbered with a sack of potatoes. I hit the floor. Hard. My head spun. My brain screamed to get up, but my body was having no part of it.

The beast towered over me, then swooped down to take a bite.

Instead of its teeth tearing into my flesh, I was pummeled with Deb's groaning, limp body still stuffed in its mouth.

Confused or frustrated, the creature whipped its head from side to side, flailing Deb around. It was a sickening display seeing another human being viciously thrashed about like a dog's rope toy.

Deb's blood and the reptile's saliva splashed everywhere.

It attacked again, hammering Deb into me. I fought back—punching, kicking—but in the confusion, every other blow struck the young woman in the face.

"Ooh! Shit! Sorry, Deb!" I kept repeating idiotically.

With the woman still stuck in its jaws, the creature rose to its full height, then plunged down.

I rolled out of the way and Deb face-planted onto the hard floor with a sickening crack. The sound reminded me of a home run hit with a wooden bat.

While her brains remained on the floor like a shattered jar of strawberry preserves, Deb rose back into the air, puppeteered by the thing. She gurgled a death rattle between broken teeth and crimson ribbons of drool. It wasn't until the top of her head hung open—and empty—that she finally stopped making noises.

I immediately turned away and threw up.

The creature let off a muffled scream.

I rolled over and saw Juan spearing the thing in the back, luring it away from me.

While spinning to face its threat, the beast whipped Deb's corpse at Juan. He stepped back, narrowly missing a blow from her broken arm that now bent backward at the elbow.

Lidia and Kyra suddenly appeared at my side, pulling me to my feet.

"You okay?" Kyra asked.

I nodded like a simpleton.

We watched Juan backpedal while bobbing and weaving around the station to keep his distance from the giant reptile. Amazingly, he looked like he'd done this before. Then I remembered his belt buckle and how he was the 1985 Fort Worth Stockyards champion. He'd probably been bucked off enough bulls to know, firsthand, how to dodge ornery, fifteen-hundred-pound beasts.

He jabbed at the creature, but it knocked the broomstick from his grasp.

"Got it!" Kyra said. She raced forward and dove over a railing, then landed in a tuck and roll next to the spear. When she popped up, she had the weapon in her hand.

"Think fast!" she told Juan and tossed it back to him.

Hearing her voice, the creature spun for Kyra, and Deb's limp body whipped around and nearly clubbed her.

Kyra screamed, dropped, and did a back roll out of the way.

Juan stabbed the beast in the shoulder to draw its attention off her.

"We have to help!" Lidia said.

Someone whistled behind us.

We turned and saw Todd standing beside a large, aluminum trash receptacle. He pointed at the bin and waved us over.

As Juan moved closer to the edge of the elevated platform, Todd, Kyra, and I charged the creature with the trash can, carrying it horizontally across our chests like a giant shield. Lidia leaned over the bin, the sharp end of her broomstick leading the way, ready to spear the thing if it turned around before we had a chance to ram it from behind.

Juan saw our approach and, realizing our plan, lured the creature closer to the outer railing. Beyond it was a fifteen-foot drop into a large fenced in area. If the fall didn't kill it, we could at least corral it.

Thinking it had Juan cornered, the reptile lunged at him. He ducked and sidestepped it, then plunged his spear into its pale gut.

A second later, we plowed into the thing with the trash

can and knocked the beast into the railing.

It let out a muffled scream and threw its head back. Deb's mangled face flopped over the litter bin, her glazed, hemorrhaged eyes staring down at us.

Kyra and I whimpered at the sight of our dead co-worker.

We continued pushing, using the trash can as a barrier.

Lidia stabbed its neck while Juan twisted his spear in deeper.

As they pinned it in place, we pulled the trash can back and rammed forward again. The creature's legs flew out from under it, and the beast, along with Deb, flipped over the railing.

Completely gassed, we dropped the trash can, staggered back, and fought to catch our breath.

I peered over the edge and saw the creature below, laying on its side, convulsing.

Something had a hold of it. Stretching out from under the dock, a tentacle-like thing coiled around the giant lizard's hind quarters and began slowly reeling it in.

From the opposite direction, a small army of ant-like things the size of Chihuahuas burst out of the shadows. The beasties swarmed both the reptile and Deb's partially consumed corpse, hanging out of the lizard's mouth.

A struggle ensued, then Deb and the giant reptile finally parted ways with a wet, tearing sound.

The enormous lizard was pulled by the tentacle one way, and Deb, the other.

As the small army of insects marched her bouncing head and torso back into the darkness from which they came, Deb's lifeless, bulging eyes stared up at me. Her outstretched arm bobbed about as if waving a final farewell.

Then she was gone.

"Dear Lord," Kyra said from over my shoulder.

Apparently, she'd also witnessed Deb's gruesome departure and immediately leaned over, placing her hands on her knees.

"I'm so gonna puke."

Deb's glasses fell out of her shirt pocket and hit the floor.

Kyra kicked them away, covered her face, and sobbed.

I rubbed her shoulder, a token gesture of solidarity for what we'd experienced. There were no words that could provide consolation.

Juan and Lidia had their arms around each other.

Todd leaned on his spear, his eyes pointed down.

"Hey," I said to him. "Thanks for jumping in, man."

He looked up and shrugged.

I paused and did a double take at Kyra's back. "Hold on. You... ah... you got a little something..."

I peeled off a cold, spongy piece of intestine from the back of her shirt. She must have picked it up during her acrobatics to retrieve Juan's spear. It stretched and snapped off her uniform like a taut rubber band.

"What the...?" she asked. "What is it?"

I shook my head, trying to avoid making a big deal out of it, and quickly tossed the entrail aside, where it landed in the shadows with a splat.

She clawed at her back, twisting her shirt, attempting to figure out what might've been there.

I patted her shoulder and said, "No-no-you're good," then walked to the opposite end of the platform.

I gazed into the darkness shrouding The Rip-Roaring Rapids and thought of Stacy.

I'm coming, sweetheart.

I ran my fingers through my hair and slowly inhaled. "Okay. We move. Now."

EIGHTEEN

WE JUMPED BACK OVER the trough, returned to the others, and told them our plan.

Although they heard us fighting for our lives with that giant lizard, they chose not to help. I couldn't blame them. Well, except Mike. Fuck Mike. If little Todd was willing to step out and risk his ass, then shit-for-brains Mike, who was nearly twice Todd's size, should've jumped in and joined the fight. Not only did he refuse, but when we reopened the closet door, he had wormed his way to the back, using an old couple, a mother and baby, and his own girlfriend as a shield. It took every ounce of self-control not to drag the coward out by his collar and throw him over the railing to those things below.

At least now we knew who could be counted on if things went south.

As for their options, I told them they could come with us or wait for help but couldn't guarantee when it would arrive.

Although the closet appeared to be a good shelter, I pointed out the huge gap between the top of its walls and the station ceiling and how anything could crawl in from above. I mentioned the miniature army we'd seen carrying Deb's body off into the dark. And the large thing under the dock with the giant tentacle. They were either lurking around, scavenging for leftovers, or the next wave was moving in.

I knew it wasn't safe for them to stay, but ultimately, it was their decision.

I informed them that Rapids had a large computer room under its dock, which housed the electronics needed to operate such a massive ride. It was climate controlled. Had concrete walls and a thick metal door that locked. The place was like a bunker, the perfect spot to hold out until help arrived. I offered to escort them over and drop them off, then would continue on for Stacy.

"And what if it's full?" Mike asked.

"What?"

"Their computer room. What if it's packed full of *their* guests?"

Kyra groaned, obviously thinking about being trapped in such a crowded place.

"Where it's so full," Mike continued, "there's no room for us. Then we'll be stuck outside. Out in the open."

"Well…" I said, searching for an answer.

"So, you expect us to risk our lives walking all the way over there, only so you can abandon us at another ride? Hmmm. I wonder how your supervisor would feel about that."

Juan guffawed. "His supervisor is probably dead. Along with most of the other people in the park, you dumb motherfucker!" Juan quickly addressed the ladies, "Pardon my language," then glared back at Mike. "Maybe if you were helping us fight earlier instead of cowering in the closet, you would've seen what's running around below us right now. You want to stay here? Fine. But you're on your own. We're leaving. You got any more stupid questions for the adults?"

Juan waited for a response.

Mike took short, shallow breaths like a frightened rabbit. His eyes darted to everyone except Juan. Before he could open his mouth with some lame retort, Vickie, his girlfriend, patted his chest.

"We should go. Gather our stuff so we can leave with them. Now."

Mike hesitated… then nodded and grabbed two large souvenir bags off the floor.

"C'mon, guys," Kyra said gently, waving them out of the closet. "Everyone hop out so we can double-check for any more weapons in there."

Anna winced while bouncing baby Ryan. Lidia noticed his tiny, neon green high-tops were untied. She approached and re-tied the toddler's shoes.

"You want me to hold him for a bit? Give your arms a rest?"

Anna appeared hesitant.

"It's okay," Lidia said. "We'll stay right here with you the entire time."

The young mother agreed, and Lidia took the toddler.

"Look at you! Such a big boy!" She bounced Ryan, making him giggle. "I remember when my little guy was this size."

Anna exhaled and forced a smile. Emotionally, she appeared to be hanging by a thread.

"They get big so fast," Lidia continued.

Anna seemed to hear Lidia but wasn't listening to what was being said. Her shoulders slumped, then she turned away and sobbed.

Lidia did her best to console her.

We scavenged for better weapons but came up empty. When Kyra held up a can of Raid found on the bottom shelf, Juan laughed so hard we had to tell him to shut up before he attracted trouble. Trust me, we were desperate enough to take the bug spray, but the can was empty.

Broomstick and squeegee handles would have to suffice.

Since no one expected an old couple or a mother with child to leap across the trough, we built a makeshift bridge with broken boards. Everyone pitched in when gathering the raw materials, even Mike, who was smart enough to keep his mouth shut during the process.

Although terrified of what lay ahead, we quickly reviewed the route we'd take, then began crossing the trough, one at a time.

NINETEEN

ACTING AS THE GUINEA pig, I crossed the bridge first. Thankfully, the coaster's track filled most of the open trough, becoming a partial barrier between us and whatever lurked below the dock.

Unfortunately, there were still large enough gaps where someone could slip through and fall twenty feet to the ground. Spots like that also meant something could reach through to snatch one of us.

Remembering the tentacle thing stretching out from under the dock, I picked up the pace until safely reaching the other side.

Kyra went next, taking it in three graceful steps as if on the balance beam.

Old Man Harry followed. At the midway point, he paused, and his knees buckled.

"Oh, geez," he said to me. He pointed into the trough and whispered, "Something's down there."

Like a deer in headlights, he remained frozen.

Before I could say, "Then move, stupid!" he scampered across and got behind me.

"What was it?" I asked.

"Something large. We heard everything is bigger in Texas but, gee-whiz, this is getting ridiculous."

I eyed him, unsure if he was trying to make a joke. If so,

it wasn't funny.

Keeping my distance from the edge, I aimed the spear at the trough, craned my neck, and peered down into the darkness. Juan did the same from the other side. After a moment, we shrugged at each other.

"Okay. Come on," I told the others. "Move fast. But be careful."

They all crossed without further incident. Once regrouped on the other side, we moved for the entrance.

By now, the rain had stopped.

Todd, Kyra, and I led the way, with Juan and Lidia taking the rear. Because of the bond formed earlier between the two mothers, Anna and baby Ryan kept close to Lidia. The old couple was second from my trio, while Mike and Vickie remained in the middle.

The fencing along the walkway provided decent cover. Creeping down the winding path, I was hit with the harsh realization that if Stacy hadn't sought shelter in the Rapids' computer room, it would be damn near impossible to find her. If she fled the ride, she could be anywhere in the park.

My gut sank.

I had promised to get Juan and Lidia to his abuela's once we got Stacy, making it sound as casual as picking her up for a double date. If she wasn't at her ride, I knew I couldn't drag them all over the park to search for her. But I also wasn't about to leave her behind. Sorry, promise or no promise, there was zero chance I was abandoning my girl.

Okay, don't get ahead of yourself. Just get to the ride first and take it from there. Stop worrying about stuff you can't control and focus on what you can, like keeping an eye on your surroundings.

I checked to make sure everyone was okay. Kyra was eyeing the landscape to our right, Todd to our left. Old Man Harry had his arm around his wife, Patty. They both solemnly marched forward. We locked eyes for a second, and he pepped up, probably afraid I'd spotted something. I shook my head and forced a smile, assuring him it was nothing.

Unable to see the rest of the group behind the couple, I leaned over the fence until spotting Juan and Lidia in the back.

Juan ticked his head as if to say, *'Wassup?'*

I shook mine again and faced forward, scanning for anything unusual.

It wasn't until stepping off the entrance ramp that I saw exactly that.

TWENTY

MUD BLED ACROSS THE walkway perpendicular to the ride's entrance. In the past, we'd had plenty of torrential downpours that flooded the location, but it usually ushered in leaves, twigs, cigarette butts, and various litter.

Never dirt to this degree.

It was like someone shoveled a bunch of soil on the asphalt to let the rainwater wash it away. It seeped in from a connecting walkway around the corner, the same path we'd have to travel to reach Rapids.

We kept our formation, with only a few feet between each couple. I led the way to the intersection.

Ahead, pools of muddy water covered the paved walkway. Two large, empty lots flanked the path. They were reserved for life-sized holiday dioramas. Whether it was a faux Halloween graveyard or a candy cane Christmas village, the attraction drew crowds from all over the park.

Currently, both sides were simply muddy fields, but I was sure something spooky was being planned with Halloween around the corner.

In our new location, the firelight from the highway wreckage was all but lost. Thankfully, the sky had cleared considerably, allowing the full moon to reflect its silver light in puddles of water and across the wet pavement.

No threat was detected in the moonlight, but it was odd

how the earth appeared freshly tilled in both fields. Had they already begun construction on the Halloween set? I didn't recall any progress when I walked past it earlier today. Then again, who pays attention to their surroundings on a route you take every day, especially when you're on autopilot?

"You see something?" Kyra said behind me.

I didn't. But things didn't feel right. The area was too quiet. Too calm.

"We should keep moving," she said.

I glanced back at her and Todd. He nodded in agreement and pointed his chin forward.

Okay. Right. We were standing in the middle of two open fields, totally exposed, especially to those giant bats that snatched up Billy and Stan. Something could be circling above us right now, preparing to swoop in.

So, get moving. Just mosey along, make the first left at the next intersection, and go down a bit until you reach the Rapids' entrance. Then go up and get Stacy. As Kyra was prone to say, 'Easy-peasy-lemon-squeezy.' Right?

White knuckling my spear, I continued forward, scanning back and forth between the surrounding shadows and the night sky.

With each step, my confidence grew.

Once I passed the midway point, I felt pretty damn g—

"Jesus!"

I spun to Juan's outburst.

The first thing I caught was something small and green landing in the dirt beside the road.

Aside from the absolute fear on Juan and Lidia's faces, the couple appeared physically fine.

"What?!" "What is it?!"

They remained silent, staring wide-eyed at the empty field to their left.

With weapons raised, we dispersed to investigate what the hell was happening.

"No!!" "Freeze!" Juan and Lidia said.

We did as commanded and waited for an explanation.

Their lips quivered, yet no words were uttered, and their trembling hands remained in a stop gesture. They continued gawking at the empty field.

Still not spotting a threat, I peered at the next couple up, Mike and Vickie, for an answer. They looked equally confused about the reaction.

Wait.

I did a quick headcount and came up two short. Okay, our marching orders were me, Kyra and Todd, Old Couple, Mike and Vickie, then...

Oh, no. Anna and baby Ryan.

I gazed at the small green object that landed roadside moments earlier.

It was a baby's sneaker.

Ryan's neon green high-top.

Anna was missing as well.

I raised my spear skyward, then turned to Juan, who frantically shook his head and pointed at the empty field to his left.

I saw nothing there and shrugged in frustration.

Mike observed the interaction, then moved toward Juan and Lidia, who both frantically motioned for him to stop.

"Don't!" "Stop moving!" "Stay still!"

He ignored their warnings and, while still holding his stupid bags of park souvenirs, crept closer.

"Oh, c'mon!" Mike said. "Cut the horseshit and tell us what you saw. What the hell happened to the lady and her ba—"

A large patch of earth flipped up in the opposite field Juan was pointing to.

We all screamed as something enormous sprung out of the ground and pounced on Mike.

A flurry of long, hairy legs clamped around the young man and snatched him off his feet.

By the time his souvenir bags crashed to the ground, the creature reeled him back into its burrow. Then a trapdoor of dirt, with its silken underside, dropped into place, concealing any sign of the threat lurking below.

Vickie stared at the space her boyfriend occupied only seconds earlier. Then she scanned the vacant field where he'd been pulled underground.

"Mike?" She stepped toward the edge of the pavement. "Mike?!"

"Stop!" We all screamed.

Thankfully, she paused.

Old Man Harry suddenly blurted something.

"What?" I asked.

"I said... it's a Ctenizidae." He pointed at his wife. "See, Patty. All those nature shows you make fun of me for watching? They do come in handy. At least I'm learning something. It's not like you and your soap operas—"

"Oh, my God!" Kyra whispered. "Would you just tell us what the hell it is?!"

"Trapdoor spider," Harry said. "Ctenizidae is a small family of mygalomorph spiders. They construct burrows with a cork-like trapdoor made of soil, silk, and—"

"How do we get away from it?" Juan said.

"Can we make a run for it?"

"Or are we, like, standing on its web?"

"Well..." Harry scratched his chin and nervously tapped his foot on the pavement. "I can't quite recall if they're attracted to sound. Or is it vibrations? It could be any sort of movemen—"

In the original field Juan had been pointing to earlier,

the earth popped up behind Harry.

An enormous shadow leaped onto the road, then snapped back.

A second later, the old man was gone, and a silken trapdoor fell back into place.

We all screamed again, except for Patty and Vickie.

"Mike?" Vickie said, seemingly oblivious to Harry's demise happening over her shoulder.

Patty wandered to the opposite side of the road to search the other field.

"Harry?"

Obviously in shock, the women seemed unable to accept the grim fate of their partners.

"Mike?"

"Harry? Hon?"

They slowly paced the road, seeking any sign of their loved ones.

"Ladies! Please!! Stop moving!"

I checked how much farther we had to go before clearing the fields. About fifteen yards. Thirty for Juan and Lidia, unless they retreated the way we came. But by doing so, they'd have to travel at least a half mile in the opposite direction, looping around two other rides before they could meet up with us at the Rapids' entrance.

And God only knew what'd be waiting for them along that dark stretch.

Patty stepped off the pavement and onto the wet soil.

"No-no-no-no," Kyra said.

She went for the old woman, but Todd grabbed Kyra's arm and pulled her back.

"What are you doing? We have to help her."

Todd shook his head and pointed a few yards in front of Patty, where a section of the ground rippled.

It was a trapdoor of muddy silk that covered another

spider's lair.

"Please, ma'am," I said. "Come back to the road. But please do it very, *very* slowly."

Patty ignored me.

"Ma'am. Please come back!"

There was an awkward silence, then Vickie came up behind the old woman.

"Your husband is gone. So is my Mike."

She extended her hand to Patty.

With a quivering voice, Vickie said, "C'mon. We have to go. We need to get someplace safe. They'd want us to do that."

The older woman lowered her head and wiped away tears, then shambled over and embraced Vickie. They approached us with their arms around each other.

Juan and Lidia cautiously followed a few yards behind.

I searched the landscape for any movement.

"That's it. Come on. Slow and steady."

The ground shot up. An enormous spider lunged out of a fourth burrow and pounced on Patty, grabbing her over the head.

The woman folded under the impact, the air exploding from her lungs in a guttural groan.

The attack happened so quickly that Vickie didn't have time to pull away. With their arms still entwined, Vickie was wrenched off her feet alongside Patty.

Before the pair got yanked into the ground, a trapdoor flipped open on the other side of the road.

Like a hairy jack-in-the-box, another spider popped out.

It latched onto Vickie and violently ripped the two women apart in midair.

Patty went in one lair, Vickie, the other.

Both trapdoors dropped simultaneously.

Seconds later, their muffled screams from underground

broke off.

We were sitting ducks.

I was about to convince everyone we needed to run for it when they grabbed me.

"Move-Move-Move!" Juan yelled, pulling me along.

Todd also had a hold of me. Lidia and Kyra led the way, somehow passing me during the chaos.

Once I picked up the pace, they let go, and we hauled ass for the intersection ahead.

TWENTY-ONE

WITH EACH THUNDEROUS STEP across the pavement, my skin crawled, and my heart raced, knowing at any moment a patch of earth would flip up to unleash another giant spider.

I focused on the road ahead and prayed there wouldn't be movement in my periphery.

A few agonizing seconds later, we bolted into the safety of the intersection, then slowed down and gathered at a large, rock-faced wall. We pressed our backs against it and struggled for breath as quietly as possible.

Kyra wiped away tears and whimpered. "They... they're all dead. Even the baby."

Juan put his arm around Lidia, who rubbed Kyra's back, trying to provide what little comfort she could.

I avoided eye contact. *I told those people they weren't safe staying in that closet.* My overwhelming guilt poured out.

"This is all my fault. I shouldn't have made them come. I'm sorry. I'm so sorry."

"You didn't make us do anything," Todd said. (It startled me to hear him speak again.) "We knew the risk."

"No-no-no-no-no," I said, pointing back to the death-trap we'd barely escaped. "I killed them. I did that. I led them there. I'm responsible." I couldn't catch my breath fast enough.

Juan rushed over, pulled me out of earshot, and got in my face.

"Get your shit together, amigo. We're counting on you to get us outta here. Remember?"

"But I-I-I got everyone killed."

"No. You didn't."

I shook my head, locked eyes with him, and blurted, "Stacy's pregnant."

"Who?"

"Stacy! My girlfriend! Remember? The one we're trying to reach?"

"Oooh." He stepped back and smiled. "Well, congrats, tiger." Then he paused and gave me a second glance. "Right?"

I didn't respond. Didn't know the honest answer anymore. But it was the first time I'd spoken of the pregnancy to someone other than Stacy.

"Look, please keep it between us. We don't want anyone else to know. I'm only telling you, so you know why it's important that we go get her. This isn't about some girl I went on a few dates with. Or some chick I'm trying to impress." I stepped closer. "We've been dating for nearly two years. We love each other. She's pregnant with my kid. I'm absolutely terrified, and not just because of all this tonight. But for our future. After tonight."

"Dude. I get it. Chill."

"I just want you to know I'm not risking all of our lives for some piece of ass."

"Okay! I heard you the first time. Now chill the hell out. We'll get you to your girl so you guys can start planning for the future. In the meantime, Lidia and I made a promise to you, just like you made one to us. We get your girl, then you take us to our kid. Right?"

I nodded.

"Good. Then let's quit yapping and go find her so I can hold my lil' hijo. Okay?"

"Okay. But like I said, please keep what I told you between us."

"Of course."

He threw his arm over my shoulder and walked me back to the group.

Once we rejoined them, he whispered something in Lidia's ear. She stared at me, and her eyes lit up.

"Awwww!" she said, then smiled and mouthed, *Congrats.*

Damn. So much for Juan keeping a secret. I gave him the stink eye and spun away to avoid drawing any more attention to the matter.

Moments later, we huddled along the sandstone wall at the far end of The Rip-Roaring Rapids. Beyond the barrier, the ride's faux river was eerily quiet and far from rip-roaring. Without power, the pumps were off, creating a stagnant channel of water throughout the attraction that ran about six feet deep.

Our best bet was to use the wall for cover and keep someone on the lookout for attacks from above. We would take the exit ramp—the shortest route to the dock—and head to the employee stairs, located just past their control booth. Those stairs led under the dock and to the computer room.

Although Todd opted to join us on our journey out of the park, we still had to check the computer room for Stacy. If she wasn't there, we'd have to search the SP towers along the ride.

"So, what now, chief?" Juan said.

Before going over the plan, I asked Kyra to listen carefully and correct me on anything I got wrong. She knew Rapids after pulling a few doubles there to work with some guy she once had a crush on. In any case, she was familiar with the backstage layout. Kyra listened and offered a tweak here and there but thought my plan was solid.

Juan and Lidia gave me a wary look when I got to the part about searching the ride. They just wanted to get to their boy, make sure he and his abuela were okay. I told them if we didn't run into trouble, we should be in and out in ten minutes. They reluctantly agreed.

I'm glad no one asked what we'd do if Stacy wasn't at the ride. I still had no answer for that.

But one thing was certain: I wasn't leaving the park without her.

Behind us, a chittering echoed out of the darkness near The Cave, an indoor water ride mimicking a spelunker tour with miniature pontoon boats. We ducked around the corner for cover, then peeked out.

Farther down, shadows slid across the walkway.

Squelching sounds, like wet footsteps, slapped the asphalt. There was a bellowing growl. Then a loud splash.

Whatever it was, it apparently claimed squatter's rights to the smaller water ride.

As silence settled back over the area, we waited in the dark, listening for any additional threats.

I took a deep breath and addressed the group.

"Okay. I'll lead the way. We move along the wall. Todd, you keep an eye out for anything above. Juan, watch our backs. Ladies, cover our side."

Once everyone nodded, I said, "All right. Let's rock."

TWENTY-TWO

SHE'D BEEN MY LIFE for nearly two years. Both my first thought upon waking and the last before drifting asleep. On the days we didn't see each other, we talked on the phone for hours.

Since I didn't have a line in my room, I used the phone in the kitchen. To get a little privacy, I'd stretch its cord around the corner and into the dining room, where I'd lay on the floor and talk.

We used to laugh our asses off whenever her dad would pick up the phone in another room and start dialing without checking to see if it was already in use.

It usually went like this:

A distinct click, telling us someone just got on the line.

We immediately stop our conversation. Is someone trying to eavesdrop?

Stacy: "I'm on the phone."

Nothing.

Stacy: "I'm on the phone! Would you please hang u—"

She's cut off by deafening DTMF tones as her father dials.

Stacy shouts into the phone during the pause between each key punch.

"I'm on—" It cuts her off.

She tries again, quicker. "I'm on the pho—"

BEEEEEP.

Frustrated, she gives up.

We wait until he finally hits that magical seventh digit.

Only now does he raise the phone to his ear... but doesn't hear the line trilling.

"Hello?" he asks, thinking maybe whomever he's called already answered.

"Dad?" (Frustration in her voice.)

"Hello?" (Confusion in his.)

"Dad?"

"Stacy Anne? Is that you?"

(I'm trying not to laugh because Stacy's an only child. Who else would call him 'Dad'?)

"Duh! Of course, it's me! I'm using the phone. Would you please hang up?"

"You've been on it all day. Others need to use it. Get off so I can make a call." (a pause) "Who you talking to? Daniel?"

"Hi, Mr. Patterson!"

"Hi, Daniel. I swear you kids are joined at the hip. Hang up and talk tomorrow. She'll still be here."

"Yes, sir."

Stacy: "Fine."

He listens, waiting for us to hang up.

"Dad, could you at least get off so we can say goodbye?"

"Fine. Make it quick!"

The phone slams down.

I burst out laughing.

Stacy exhales. A second later, she giggles uncontrollably.

"My dad is *such* a dork!"

I thought about those goofy little exchanges whenever she wasn't around, and they always made me smile.

Then there were times—whether at the movies or chilling with friends— when she'd reach over and grab my hand.

Physically, I didn't think we could get any closer, already sitting side by side, my arm around her, her head nestled on my shoulder. Almost without thinking, she'd reach for my hand and hold it in her lap. Sometimes Stacy would look over and silently smile, but mostly she'd remain focused on whatever we were watching or listening to.

That's when I realized something subconscious was happening.

Through such a simple gesture, we were connecting at an even deeper level. It probably sounded silly to some, or to others, that I was majorly p-whipped, but when I noticed the little things like that, it made me love her even more.

It was just our connection, almost like two halves coming together to make one.

My eyes flickered at the analogy.

Two halves joining to make one? I guess you could say we kind of did that, huh?

Then I sighed and wanted to kick myself. How could I have suggested what I did earlier on break? Because I was scared and weak and looking for an easy way out.

I had failed her.

No wonder there was pain and disappointment in her eyes.

Since those things first crawled out of the earth, my chest constantly ached knowing Stacy was somewhere out there in danger and that I couldn't be there for her.

That was beyond my control.

But after tonight, I had a choice to be there for her and the baby. She had made it very clear she was having it with or without me.

So, how about it? What was I going to do?

I still held a grudge against my father for leaving us. Always swore I'd never be like him. I knew how it felt to grow up without a dad and witnessed the strain it put on my mom as a single parent.

Why would I ever choose to do that to Stacy?

To our kid?

Look, it all boiled down to this: Although I was scared shitless and the last thing I wanted was to be eaten alive, I was still out there, risking my life, willing to battle any fucking thing that got in my way to reach this woman.

I realized the fear of living without her was greater than any fear of death.

So, I had to ask myself, what was I so scared of before the power went out?

How much more terrifying could it be to live life raising a beautiful child with the woman I love?

Her father's words echoed in my mind. "*Hang up and talk tomorrow. She'll still be here.*"

Never again would I take such words for granted.

TWENTY-THREE

APPROACHING THE RAPIDS' ENTRANCE, I raised my hand for everyone to stop. Instead, they kept moving and knocked me down, making us the lamest search party ever.

Todd helped me up and dusted me off while the others asked what I'd seen.

Nothing. I'd only paused to scope out the entrance and exit in the distance for anything suspicious.

All seemed quiet, which was of little comfort considering the last time we let our guard down, over half of our group was picked off by giant spiders leaping out of the ground.

Inching closer, we arrived at a blacktop filled with concession stands and game booths.

A smashed funnel cake stand was set ablaze by an overturned deep fryer. Cooking oil crept out, sizzling and smoking toward a pile of intestines laying on the asphalt.

Thankfully, firelight from the burning rubble pushed back the darkness.

Silhouettes of stuffed animals hung from the rafters of various game booths while others lined their back walls.

Within all the plush toys, there were the usual teddy bears, dragons, unicorns, and other cartoon characters, but one stood out from the pack. It was oddly shaped, coated in patchy hair, and crowned with a half dozen mirror balls that looked more like—

Eyes.

My heart rocketed into my throat.

The stuffed animals were thrown aside and something the size of a large dog burst out of the shadows.

I recoiled, bounced off a lamppost, and stumbled.

The mutated spider scampered out of the booth in a flurry of long, segmented legs.

Before the creature could engulf me, it lurched back. As spears pierced its body, it jerked one way, then the other, before being slammed into the booth wall.

While Lydia and Todd kept it pinned in place, Kyra leaped onto the game counter and plunged her broomstick into the arachnid's head.

Juan and I jumped in and stabbed it repeatedly.

"Oh, c'mon!" Juan said, spearing it faster and faster. "Would you freakin' die already?!"

It finally collapsed, flipped onto its back, and drew its twitching legs inward and upward.

Flustered and gasping for air, we stared at each other in amazement and admiration over our hardcore accomplishment.

Moments later, I darted to the exit. Its ramp had only two turns where something could be waiting. Beyond that, it was a straight shot up to the dock.

A glance at the group confirmed they were armed and ready. Todd stepped up beside me to help lead the way; Kyra and Lidia remained center and fluid; Juan took the rear to prevent a sneak attack.

"Okay," I said. "Everyone stay sharp."

Then, off we went. Slowly.

At the first turn, Todd fell back to let me peek around the corner. I spotted something a few yards out and held up an index finger. Once everyone stopped, I went for another look.

It was a corpse. Well, the upper half of one. It had been ravaged. Viciously torn apart and strewn about.

"It's okay," I whispered. "It's only a dead body."

The second the words crossed my lips, I realized how messed up the statement was and how we would need years of therapy once the night was over.

I waved them on. As we approached the corpse in a single file line, I made the mistake of looking down.

It was a young man. His chest was ripped open, and his stomach hollowed out, the organs and entrails picked clean. The top of his head was gone, bitten off. Only a small glob of brain matter clung to his brow. One hand gripped a toddler's blood-spattered shoe.

I immediately thought of Anna and baby Ryan.

Todd nudged me to keep moving.

I pressed on but couldn't shake the image of the dead man.

The tiny shoe in his hand meant he was either a father or had jumped in to protect somebody else's child when predators descended upon the ride. And now he was gone, reduced to a husk of bones and gristle, cracked open, torn apart, and picked clean like some rotisserie chicken.

His death mask slowly faded but was quickly replaced by those who'd died that night. Their faces strobed like ghostly images glimpsed after a camera flash.

Stan, Billy, Greg, and Deb.
Old Man Harry and Patty.
Mike and Vickie.
Anna and baby Ryan.
All taken too soon.
Before I knew it, we reached the deserted dock.
The burning funnel cake stand from below cast enough

light to view our surroundings. There were body parts scattered about, but no more faces of the dead that would haunt me for years to come. The floor was streaked with blood. Kills were dragged elsewhere to be devoured within the shadows. Some trails went to the edge of the trough. Others led off the dock or into the queue house.

We moved slightly closer to the trough's edge and gazed into the murky water reflecting the full moon.

I shuddered at the thought that something was probably beneath the surface, staring back.

A docked boat provided safe passage to the other side.

I went first.

Stepping onto its padded seat, a high-pitched shriek sounded near my foot. With a hammering heart, I leaped back as a bunch of dark shapes the size of large cockroaches swirled around the craft's interior.

Squealing like stuck piglets, they scuttled up and out the other side, then dispersed in various directions.

The fact none of us bothered to check the boat's interior before crossing was a glaring reminder of how luck had played a major role in our survival so far.

I exhaled and waited for any more surprises.

Moving forward, we all crossed to the other side.

Kyra pointed to the far end of the dock.

"Control booth is there. The stairs leading down to the computer room just past it."

The shadowy booth filled a recess within the rock wall and appeared to be all smashed to hell.

I stepped forward, and Kyra grabbed my arm.

"Wait," she said, then turned to Todd, Lidia, and Juan. "The computer room is the white metal door at the bottom of the stairs. Just to the left. Got it?"

The trio appeared slightly confused.

"I'm telling you this because if anything happens to me

or Danny along the way, you guys need to know where to run."

"Don't talk like that," Juan said. "Nothing's gonna happen to either of you with us around."

Lidia and Todd nodded in agreement.

It was supposed to be one of those moments where their reassurance boosted our confidence, but such bravado meant squat after seeing how vulnerable we were against those things.

Then again, we gave that spider at the game booth a real ass whoopin.'

Kyra spun me around, patted my shoulder, and gently nudged me forward. Todd came up beside me. With spears raised, we crossed into the shadows from the overhanging rocks.

I cautiously peeked into the control booth and found it empty.

Beyond the booth, the walkway narrowed, forcing us to fall back into a single file formation. We kept our backs flush with the wall to put as much distance between us and the trough as possible. Although we had yet to see anything in the water, I sensed that's where the real threat lurked.

Once the platform expanded again, we gathered around the spiral staircase and peered down.

The flicker of firelight burned below.

"I'll go down for a peek," I said. "You guys stay here."

"What?" Juan asked, obviously questioning my sanity.

"If there's something down there, these stairs are too narrow for everyone to rush back up all at once. It's best to send a scout."

"I'll go," Todd said. "You're needed to guide everyone out of the park."

I shook my head. "Kyra knows the way, too. So, everyone chill and I'll be right back. Promise."

With great reservation, I took a step down. Then another. After a few more, I ducked below deck to look around.

The metal door to the computer room was at the foot of the stairs like Kyra said. It was dented and had large claw marks running its length but was still intact.

I descended a few more steps and surveyed the area.

A section of the wooden fence at the front of the ride was smashed inward, allowing firelight through. My eyes darted around to make sure whatever caused the damage wasn't still there.

While the station was heavily fortified to keep guests out of restricted areas, the actual ride was a botanical landscape filled with trees, flowers, thick foliage, and large sandstone rocks. It all created the illusion that riders were on an isolated adventure, traveling along white-water rapids.

The open area ahead was used for dry storage and ride maintenance. A paved walkway entered the woods and led to the riverside SPs.

Finding no threats, I softly called to the group.

"Okay, guys. Come on down."

Once we gathered around the computer room door, I rapped on it with the side of my fist. We all cringed at the loud noise, only because we'd been trying to remain stealthy for so long.

Receiving no answer, I pounded on it again. Harder.

"Hello? Anyone in there?"

After a moment, a lock clicked from the other side and the door creaked open.

TWENTY-FOUR

WE STEPPED BACK AS the door opened. Expecting to see Stacy after such a long and horrible night, my heart raced with anticipation.

Instead, some chick wearing a Rapids uniform with a neon orange visor poked her head out. Her nametag was missing. I'd seen her a few times in the canteen but never had an introduction.

She peeked past us, and once finding the coast clear, opened the door all the way.

People gathered behind her. Some held flashlights.

I quickly stepped inside and scanned the terrified faces for Stacy. There were about two dozen people there, but only a few employees, none being my girlfriend.

My heart sank.

"Stacy Patterson," I said to the employees inside. "Has anyone seen her?"

One person stepped forward. I think his name was Mark. I checked his name tag. *Max*. He sat with Stacy and I once at the canteen when they were sent on break together. Nice guy. Kind of quiet. Didn't have money for lunch, so we bought it for him. He spent most of the half hour turned away, chewing on a straw while watching the ballgame on the tube. I didn't mind since it gave me and Stacy a little privacy for our lovey-dovey talk that we knew no one else wanted to hear.

"When all this started," Max said, "she was at SP-6."

"You sure?"

"Yeah. She took my place during rotations."

Kyra appeared to be running through the SP locations in her head.

"Is it the one at the drop off?" she said. "Is that six?"

Max nodded.

The drop off was a four-story fiberglass slide running at a thirty-degree angle. It was the climax of the ride, where the boats raced down and splashed into a large pool, drenching everyone onboard.

SP-6 was stationed next to that pool.

"You remember how to get there?" I asked Kyra.

"Yeah. Once we hit the walkway," she thumbed to the cement path over her shoulder, "we go right instead of left. Start at the end. And it's the second to the last SP down." She turned to Max. "Right?"

"Correct."

I skimmed the various faces in the shadowy computer room again. They were petrified with fear. A young woman spoke up.

"Is help on the way?"

"I… I hope so." It was the only answer I could give.

"Okay then, in or out?" the visor girl asked us. She held the door wide open. "We need to shut this before any more of those things show up and try to get in."

"What's out there?" Lidia asked. "What did you see?"

"After the initial attack? Nothing. 'Cause we hid our butts in here. But we heard them. Roaming around. Scratching at the door. And then there was something big."

"Big?" Kyra said.

Visor girl nodded.

"How big?"

Shock Waves

"Big." Her eyes were as wide as saucers. "Now, c'mon! In or out?"

I hustled outside to rejoin my group.

"Last chance," visor girl said.

We stood silent.

"Okay. Fine. But please... if you find help, tell them where we are. And good luck, guys."

She slammed the door and flipped the lock.

Hit the walkway, turn right, and it's the second SP down. I was about to repeat it once more when Juan patted my chest.

"All right. You ready, sport?"

"Yeah. But I got it from here." I turned to Kyra. "Get them to the parking lot. Take the rear walkway behind The Cave until you reach the old-fashioned ice cream parlor. There's a chain-link fence behind it with a gate used for deliveries. That leads you to the employee entrance, then to parking. Take them," I pointed at Juan and Lidia, "to the wooded lot at overflow. It's the same one where that guy from Bumper Cars sat in the ant bed at the company picnic. Remember?"

Kyra nodded and winced at the recollection.

"Whoa-whoa-whoa. Time out," Juan said, interrupting.

I ignored him. "At the back of that lot, there's a brick wall. Get them to it and they'll take it from there. Got it?"

Kyra nodded again, then exhaled and opened her mouth to say something.

Before she could, I pivoted to Todd. "You go with them. Strength in numbers. Okay?"

"What the hell are you doing, man?" Juan said.

I finally addressed him and Lidia. "When y'all reach your abuela's, please take in Kyra and Todd until all this blows over."

"Nope. It ain't going down like this. We promised to get your girl first. Then you promised to lead us out of here.

That's the plan. That's what we shook on. So quit trying to be all Arnie or Sly or going all *Die Hard* on us, acting like you need to go about this alone."

"I'm not trying to be tough. I just don't want anyone else getting killed. So you can be with your kid and not orphan him."

"And we're trying to do the same for you. So you can be there for Stacy when *your* kid is born in a few months."

Juan's eyes suddenly went wide, as did mine and Lidia's.

"Oops," he said and slapped his hand over his mouth.

Lidia smacked his shoulder.

We remained silent for a beat, hoping Kyra wasn't paying attention.

Then, from over my shoulder…

"Oh. My. God! Stacy's pregnant?"

I spun around. "Please don't tell anyone. We haven't even told our parents yet. So, please, keep it a secret. Okay? Please?"

"Yeah. Okay. Umm… wow. Congratulations," she said, then gave me a second glance. "Right?"

This time, I didn't have to think about it. I smiled.

"Yeah. Absolutely."

Juan patted my shoulder.

"All right. Let's boot scoot and get your lady."

TWENTY-FIVE

ENTERING THE WOODS, WE followed the paved walkway and took a right. A few yards in, a section of the brush turned into a large, slimy trail leading to the river's edge. Not a good sign.

Then my stomach dropped at what I saw in the water.

An SP was submerged and upside down.

Kyra rushed over to me.

"It's not hers! That's SP-7. Stacy's is the next one up."

Once my lungs started working again, I inspected the damage from afar.

Safety posts were essentially beefed-up lifeguard stands, almost resembling a kid's treehouse. They had a fiberglass roof, metal railings, and an attached ladder. Inside were a chair and a phone (interior line only) to stay in contact with the control booth on the dock.

SP-7 stuck out of the flume, topsy-turvy. Its thick, wooden legs were snapped off its concrete base and pierced the stagnant water.

"Okay. I'm confused," Lidia said. "How do you guys get across to the other side? To the safety post."

"The bridge," Todd said, looking around, slightly confused.

Kyra nodded.

"So, where is it?" Lidia asked, glancing up and down the

river.

"It's gone," Kyra said.

"Gone?"

"It's supposed to be right there, but it's… just… gone."

The closest bridge had only its base intact. There were partial stairs on both sides of the river, but the walkway in between was missing. It was as if something very large swam through the channel and plowed right through it.

Bubbles suddenly rose around the sunken SP.

We jumped back and aimed our weapons in its direction.

Based on the slimy trail heading to the river, and what we'd heard earlier at The Cave, some of these things were indeed aquatic. (After all, they came from deep within the earth, where there are plenty of subterranean reservoirs.)

Juan cautiously moved for the water's edge when Lidia snatched his arm and reeled him back.

"Where do you think you're going?" she asked.

"Just looking."

"Look from here. You don't need to get any closer."

"Ya know, maybe it's whoever was working that stand."

"It's not."

"How do you know, babe?"

"Hello?!" She hollered toward the water. "Anyone need help?"

We winced as her voice echoed into the night without a reply.

"See? Not someone. Some*thing*."

Lidia was right. I started down the sidewalk for the next SP, praying we wouldn't find it the same way.

"C'mon. Let's keep moving."

We continued until something splashed in the river running parallel to us. We paused to see if it was someone needing help.

I bit my lip and fidgeted with the broomstick, knowing it was one of those damn things scavenging for food. Possibly swimming upstream toward Stacy.

I had to get ahead of it.

Growing impatient, I continued along the winding trail through the tall brush. It was foolish to wander ahead alone, but before I could do the smart thing and turn back, an intense strobing beyond the foliage caught my eye. It was like someone was using a giant welding torch.

The next turn revealed a blown power transformer sparking on top of a steep hill.

I had reached the drop off.

Normally, the four-story waterslide would be flowing, but without power to the pumps, its fiberglass surface appeared bone dry. A short containment wall and dozens of stairs ran the length of the hill on both sides.

My attention fell back to the crackling transformer mounted on top of a telephone pole. Although it provided plenty of light to see by, its incessant flashing was disorienting. Shadows leaped wildly, making it difficult to spot any looming threat.

Within all the bursts of blue light, I saw SP-6 in the distance. It stood on the opposite side of the large pool.

Beach towels and a yellow raincoat haphazardly hung over the railings, almost as if to purposely obscure the view inside. To me, the peculiar placement of the articles was proof of life. Someone was hiding in there.

My heart drummed in my chest.

Advancing a few steps, I was about to yell for Stacy when large bubbles broke the surface of the pool between us. A muffled bellow came from underwater.

The bubbles moved in my direction.

I darted back and ducked behind a tree.

The water suddenly rippled and something huge floated

in from downstream.

It was a capsized boat.

The vessels were bottom heavy to prevent them from tipping. So, whatever flipped it must've been enormous. If there were passengers onboard, they'd most likely drowned and were probably still strapped upside down in their seats. Waterlogged, bloated, and half-eaten.

"There you are!" Juan said over my shoulder. "What the hell, man?"

I shushed him and told the group about the bubbles in the water. We stared at the large claw marks raked across the boat before it floated downstream again.

Kyra came up beside me, pointed across the pool, and whispered, "That's it! That's SP-6!"

"Please tell me it's not normal for employees to hang a bunch of stuff over the railings."

"No way. Supes would have a major cow if they saw it looking all Gilligan's Island like that."

"Thank you. That's what I needed to hear."

Then, after inhaling sharply, I told everyone, "All right. I'm going across."

TWENTY-SIX

"**YOU CAN'T SWIM OVER** there," Kyra said. "Who knows what's in the water?"

Lidia nodded. "What about the bubbles you saw? And the splashing we heard earlier."

"Don't be stupid," Juan said.

"Dude," Todd said and shook his head in disapproval.

"I'm not swimming." I pointed at the slide. "I'm walking across."

"Get outta here," Kyra said. "There's another bridge two SPs up. Just cross there. It'll be much safer."

"Will it? I'll have to take the stairs up the hill, walk all that way to the bridge, cross over, walk back, and then take the stairs back down on the other side. That's a lot of ground to cover, where I could run into a lot of hungry things. Plus, like the other bridge, it might not even be there anymore."

I jabbed my finger at the slide again. "This is the shortest distance. Across."

We studied my options.

The slide leveled off at the bottom for a smooth transition into the pool, which would've made crossing there a cakewalk without the pumps on. Only now, that area was completely submerged. The high water level could've been the result of all the heavy rain or, more likely, displaced by the body mass of whatever was lurking beneath the pool's surface.

So that meant walking across a slide sloped at a thirty-degree angle. Sure, it was dangerous, but no riskier than venturing upriver in the dark to a bridge that may no longer exist.

"You know, if you slip and bust your ass, you'll slide right into that pool," Juan said. "Then you'll find out, firsthand, what's in the water."

"I'm going."

"It's a bullshit call, sport."

"What if it was Lidia trapped over there? Would you feel the same way?"

"I'm not saying that, just that it's—"

I left the conversation and marched up the steps. Of course, Juan was right about the possibility of the slide being extremely slick, which was why I would start at the top. I needed to put as much distance as possible between me and the pool at the bottom. The higher I started, the more chances I'd have to try to stop on the way down if I slipped.

The gang followed me uphill.

Once at the top, I gazed at the dark reservoir leading up to the drop off. Without the pumps on, its water level had dropped to about four feet deep and was now flush with the top of the fiberglass slide.

The water had a slight ebb and flow, with some of it trickling over the edge and down the slide, possibly from something swimming upriver.

Which meant I needed to get my ass in gear before it got any closer.

"I'll cross over and check things out," I told them, then turned to Kyra. "If anything happens to me, please get Juan and Lidia to their kid. Okay?"

She looked like she wanted to say something but only

nodded.

I eyed the water above the drop off and how it rhythmically pulsed.

Something was coming.

Then get moving and quit thinking about it!

Kyra rushed forward and got in my face.

"Okay, listen up! This is about balance. Weight distribution. Gimme that." She took my spear and tossed it to Juan. "You'll need both hands for balance. Keep your body sideways."

She grabbed my hips and forcefully twisted me around to face the slide.

I tensed, then realized she was slipping into a coaching role. As a gymnast, I'm sure she received a ton of these pep talks.

She kicked my legs until they were shoulder width apart.

I glanced at the others as if to say, '*Pfft, check* her *out.*'

Kyra shoved me. "Eyes on me!"

"Okay! Okay. Sorry!"

She pointed at my foot. "That's your main anchor. Keep most of your weight on that foot. Almost like a surfer stance. Lean uphill, and on your left foot. Move sideways. Take short steps. Before moving your left foot, dig in deep with the ball of your right one. Always make sure you're firmly anchored before moving the opposite foot. Got it?"

"Yeah."

Kyra hooted, smacked my ass, and pushed me to the slide.

"Easy-peasy-lemon-squeezy! Now show us what you got!"

After taking a second to review everything she told me, I threw a leg over the wall to test the slickness of the fiberglass, then climbed over and got into position.

Juan leaned across the wall, ready to grab me if I slipped.

The rest of the group fanned out along the length of the slide, upping my chances of being caught by at least one of them if I fell. They had their spears extended, round end out, ready for me to grab. All fine and dandy if I slipped within a few feet of the wall.

Anything beyond that, I was on my own.

Still, there they were, ready to risk their lives to save mine.

It was then that I realized if we made it out alive, we were going to be friends for life. Juan and Lidia could've easily demanded that Kyra take them to the parking lot, leaving me alone with my insane quest. Instead, they stayed and helped. The same with Kyra, who could have bailed on everyone the minute all hell broke loose. But she remained to protect the guests and fought by my side. And this Todd kid? What a fearless little dude. I planned to get his story over a feast of cheeseburgers and jumbo milkshakes.

I mean, these people were like family now. In fact, I wasn't afraid to admit I loved them like brothers and sis—

"Oh, c'mon, man!" Juan shouted.

I flinched and nearly slipped.

"I wanna see my kid! Move your ass."

Yeah! Okay. Right! I took my first step toward the other side. It was sloppy and off balanced, like the first time I roller-skated at one of our elementary school skate parties. Even worse, the strobing transformer was completely disorienting, slinging shadows every which way.

But I took it slow and steady, focusing on Juan's encouragement over my shoulder.

Making headway, my confidence grew, and I picked up the pace. When I reached the middle of the slide, the point of no return, a single splash from above caused water to spill over the edge and run past my shoes.

Glancing up to see what caused the commotion, my right foot slid forward with a loud squeak.

The breath hitched in my chest.

I squatted, shifted my weight to the left leg, dug in deep, and, thankfully, stopped. I squeezed my eyes shut and concentrated on my balance, letting my muscles either tense or relax, depending on which one needed to do what.

After regaining control of the situation, I transferred my focus to a random spot on the opposite side. Then took it slow and steady.

Once making it over, I hugged the wall and got the hell off the slide.

Juan hurled my spear over to me. I caught it and clutched it so tight my hands turned to fine porcelain.

Fear and adrenaline surged through my body. Trembling uncontrollably, I crouched out of sight with my back against the containment wall and closed my eyes.

Deep breath in. Slow exhale.

To help calm me even more, I thought of Stacy. Lying with her. Her head on my chest, her palm over my heart, her big brown eyes staring up at me. Then hearing her whisper, "I love you so much."

"Hang up and talk tomorrow. She'll still be here."

My eyes snapped open.

Gripping the spear, I sprang to my feet and started down the stairs to make damn sure that she still would be.

TWENTY-SEVEN

THE PUNGENT ODOR OF ammonia and rotting seafood grew stronger at the bottom of the stairs.

I noticed that the gang had followed me down on the other side of the pool. Although unable to do squat if the shit hit the fan, they were at least looking out for me, ready to warn of any threat that might be creeping about.

The SP stood ten yards ahead. To its right was the giant pool at the bottom of the slide that fed back into the river; to its left, a chain-link fence threaded with bamboo slats. A large section of the fence had been trampled and crushed inward. A trail of slime ran past the SP and into the pool. Whatever crashed through must've rushed into the water and might be submerged there.

To make matters worse, SP-6 was about ten feet from the water's edge. Having seen enough nature shows of crocodiles lunging out of calm waters to grab some unsuspecting animal, I knew this wasn't good.

Hell, I'd already witnessed things diving out of the sky and jumping out of the earth, so why not water?

Now, I could stand there all night and ponder the endless dangers around me, or I could move my ass and go see if my girlfriend was up there.

Rushing to the base of the SP, I threaded the broomstick through a belt loop, freeing both hands to climb the ladder. Scrambling up, my foot slipped off a wet rung, and I nearly hit my chin on another.

"Dammit!"

So much for remaining stealthy.

I clung to the ladder, whipped my head back and forth like a spooked owl, then glanced up and flinched.

Someone peered down at me from out of the booth, their long blonde hair cascading in front of their face.

"Danny?!"

Hearing Stacy's voice, my heart pounded triple-time.

I scrambled up and dove into her arms. We collapsed to our knees in a back-breaking hug.

"My God," she whispered. "I was so worried about you, baby! Are you okay?! What's happening?! Where did these things come from?"

After I filled her in on what I knew, she told me how she'd just rotated and was settling into her post when there was an explosion somewhere in the distance. Then, as a boat went down the slide, the power went out, and the pumps shut off. Without the necessary jet flow, the vessel floated idly back and forth in the large pool, slowly bouncing off the sides like a real-life game of Pong.

She used her megaphone to tell the guests that all was fine and that the power would soon be restored. To put them even more at ease, she climbed down from the stand with a flashlight and stood at the water's edge so they wouldn't feel alone.

But the longer the power remained out, the more restless they became. So, as a distraction, she coaxed them into singing Bobby McFerrin's "Don't Worry, Be Happy." At key points in the song, she even did the melodic cuckooing through her megaphone, much to the guests' amusement.

Shortly after they completed the song and someone requested another, all hell broke loose.

The ground rumbled, and the water rippled from the approaching stampede. Explosions from the highway were quickly followed by screams within the park. Then various creatures leaped over or scuttled down the Rapids' exterior walls. They landed on the opposite side of the pool, dove into the water, or jumped onto the boat, attacking the terrified guests.

"There was nothing I could do for them," Stacy said with tears in her eyes. "The boat was too far away. Then those things started swimming across and coming out of the water. So, I booked it back up into the SP and hid. I needed to protect our…"

She covered her flat belly. I placed my hand over hers, interlacing our fingers.

"Whatever I had in here, I hung over the sides to remain out of sight." She lowered her head. "I wanted to find you, but I was too scared to go out there alone. They were everywhere. So, I hid here and prayed. For you. For everyone. I'm sorry, Danny. I'm so sorry." She sobbed and melted to the floor.

I held her tight. "Don't be. You did all you could. And those prayers helped. Trust me."

I waited until she stopped crying, then lifted her chin.

"I need to tell you something. Like, right now."

"What? What is it?"

"I am so sorry about what I suggested earlier on break. It's not what I want. Not anymore. I want us to have this baby. Move in together. Get married. The whole deal. Because one thing this horrible night has taught me is that I love you so, *so* much. And I can't imagine a life without you."

"You mean it?"

"Absolutely."

"Even if we were going to have twins?"

"Wait. What? We... we're gonna have twins?" I was seconds from shitting a brick.

"How do I know? I haven't even seen a doctor yet. I'm just saying—"

"Yes! Even if we were having twins. One baby. Twins. Triplets. A whole litter. Whatever. Let's do this. We'll figure it all out later."

We kissed.

"Okay. Now we gotta get out of here."

She wiped away tears. "What's your plan? Like I said, these things are everywhere."

"Kyra and I came with a group. We all came to get you." I rose to my knees. "Come on. I should've already let them know you're here and okay."

Stacy pulled me back down.

"Wait. Just don't yell. Whatever is in the pool is attracted to sound. And maybe movement. Some guy was walking by the water's edge, yelling for someone, when it sprung out and grabbed him."

"What did?"

"Some sort of tongue or tentacle thing. It all happened so fast. I didn't even have time to warn him. It just shot out and pulled him under."

Thinking of the trapdoor spiders, I shuddered.

"I'm telling you these things are everywhere. Especially underwater. And something enormous got in not too long ago."

"You see it?"

"You kidding? I was too afraid to move. Let alone peek out."

I thought about my group. Although they'd been vigilant about staying away from the water's edge, they needed to be warned of the imminent danger.

"Just stay low and peek out over the top," she said.

"That's all. Okay?"

I followed her lead and, upon seeing the group, pointed at my girl with a beaming smile while giving an enthusiastic thumbs up.

They sighed in relief and waved their approval.

Stacy pressed an index finger to her lips, pointed to the water, and shooed everyone back.

They complied and retreated a few yards.

When Juan motioned for us to rejoin the group, I shook my head and beckoned them to us.

He surveyed the steep slide they'd all have to cross and scoffed.

"I gotta tell them that the hole in the fence over here is a shortcut. Then they'll come." I cupped my hands around my mouth and took a deep breath to shout over.

A monstrous roar came from the other side of the three-story rock wall that separated us from Rapids' dock.

"Oh, boy. That sounded big! I thought you said it went into the water."

"It did. This is something else!"

TWENTY-EIGHT

SOMETHING MOVED QUICK AND heavy, not caring about stealth. If it hadn't already given away its location with a roar, then the stomping across gravel and the shaking treetops over the dividing wall were a good indication of its whereabouts.

The gang raced for shelter, ducking behind trees to flee the commotion happening over their shoulders.

It suddenly stopped as fast as it began, and everything appeared calm.

Stacy grabbed my hand. We eyed the enormous wall across from the pool and strained to hear what was happening on the other side.

There was heavy breathing and snorting.

Then it all went to shit after another roar, which was followed by thunderous pounding against metal.

I thought of the scarred computer room door and how visor girl said something tried to get in earlier.

It must have returned.

Metal crumpled, as if being folded or peeled back. There were shrieks of terror and pleas for divine intervention. Footsteps, too fast for anything human, scurried through the gravel.

Within seconds, the blood-curdling screams cut off and an eerie silence blanketed the area.

Then the feeding began.

Moist tearing. Crunching bones. Animalistic grunts of satisfaction.

In the distance, an eerie howl tapered into a cicada-like chitter that grew louder. Whatever it was, it sounded like it was heading our way, possibly attracted to the feast.

I shouted to the group, "C'mon! There's a shortcut over here to the parking lot. Hurry!"

This time, they didn't refuse. Backtracking meant running directly into whatever was eating the people from the computer room. Staying put meant an introduction to what might be approaching.

They ran up the steps as the strobing transformer projected their shadows across us. We followed them up when Stacy grabbed my hand.

"Wait! I got an idea!"

She pulled me back down the stairs and grabbed a pool skimmer hanging on the side of the SP. The hollow aluminum staff was about eight feet long, but pressing two prongs at one end released an inner pole that extended it another four feet.

Rushing back up, we took two stairs at a time and held out the skimmer. Stacy stood up front while I acted as the anchor. Unfortunately, even with its mesh basket still attached, the pole only reached about a third of the way. Still, it was better than nothing.

"If you're about to slip, dive for the basket!"

Juan climbed out first, followed by Lidia, then Kyra, and finally, Todd.

As they began crossing, a loud gelatinous *blurp* came from the pool below.

Everyone paused to look at the large bubble breaking

the surface.

"Um. What is that?" I whispered to Stacy.

Before she could respond, more gigantic bubbles roiled the water, sending up debris.

Looking closer, I saw gnawed body parts—arms, legs, someone's head—bobbing across the pool's surface.

Then the water went still.

With a horrified expression, I glanced at Stacy, then to the others, who shot me a look that read, '*What the hell did you get us into?*'

I shrunk under their stare.

"Everyone, stay focused," Kyra said. "Remember, your left foot is your anchor. Just move one foot at a time. Slow and easy. Slow and easy."

They continued shuffling toward the skimmer.

To the right, the cicada chitter got louder. To our left, whatever was submerged in the pool belched up more body parts. And straight ahead, the beast eating the people from the computer room became even more unruly, roaring and raking the other side of the stone wall as if trying to climb over.

Water splashed above and trickled down the slide. I looked up to see what was there, but when Juan slipped, my eyes snapped back to him.

He hissed and struggled to find his balance.

I held my breath.

A moment later, he steadied himself.

"You good?" Lidia said.

He exhaled. "Am now, babe. Thanks for asking."

As they resumed their migration, I checked above to make sure the coast was still clear… and nearly had a heart attack.

Along the horizon of the aqueduct, eight bulging eyes popped out of the water and peered down the slide.

Stacy must've felt my jolt and turned around.

I motioned for her to—nonchalantly—look above. She did and went bug-eyed but thankfully kept quiet.

The last thing the gang needed to know was that there was something in the water watching them.

"What. The. Fuck!?" Juan said.

Welp. So much for that.

His reaction caused the others to follow his gaze.

They looked up and gasped.

More water spilled over the edge.

"C'mon!" I said. "Just keep moving!"

At the lip of the reservoir, a thick tentacle flopped out of the water and onto the top of the slide. After writhing around, it elongated and began descending.

"Guys! Focus on me and Stacy. Just keep moving! You're almost here!"

That was a lie. Juan, who was in the lead, was a little over halfway. At the rear, Todd was only a quarter of the way out.

The tentacle stretched its length but came up a few feet short of reaching anyone.

So, a thicker, larger one sprung out of the water. Then another.

"Come on, guys!" Stacy yelled. "C'mon-c'mon!"

The tentacles curled into the air and slapped down with a heavy thud. Their suckers adhered to the fiberglass. They flexed and strained.

Whatever they stemmed from, rose out of the water.

The dark mass teetered on the lip of the slide, then slung forward and shot down… heading directly for Kyra.

TWENTY-NINE

THE BEST WAY TO describe the creature was a turtle-like thing nestled on a squirming bed of tentacles. Its telescoping head appeared to have only a slit for a mouth until the horizontal crease snapped open like a fleshy umbrella, revealing pink inner cheeks coated in barbed fangs.

It rocketed down the slide—tentacles flailing, cheeks flapping—hell-bent on grabbing Kyra.

At the last second, she did a jump tuck over the creature and managed to land gracefully on the thirty-degree slant.

The thing zipped away empty-handed and splashed into the dark waters below.

Any hint of accomplishment on Kyra's face quickly turned to terror when another creature flung itself over the edge and dive-bombed Todd.

Instead of sidestepping the thing (and risk taking out Kyra), the kid dove over it.

As the beast shot under him, Todd landed hard, belly flopping onto the slide.

The creature flew down and skipped across the pool… right into the waiting mouth of an eel-like behemoth rising from the depths.

Like a gigantic bear trap, its gaping maw snapped shut over the shelled creature, then it dove back under the surface with its catch.

Todd struggled to rise, slipped again, and fell flat. As more water rushed between them, Kyra shuffled closer to help.

The top of the slide writhed with tentacles, all creeping their way down.

Another shelled creature slung itself out and over.

Todd rolled sideways to dodge it and accidentally took out Kyra's legs, knocking her off her feet.

She sailed over him and made a hard landing that put her last in line.

The monster soared past them, splashed into the pool, and was immediately devoured by the waiting eel-thing.

Witnessing Kyra and Todd's struggle, my heart both raced and ached for them.

Then Kyra went first, shrieking, clawing, and kicking for purchase to stop her descent.

"No!" I screamed.

Todd spun on his belly and snatched her outstretched hand. She stopped temporarily, but her momentum jarred him loose from his dry spot, then both started down the slide.

"Form a chain!" Juan said. "Form a chain!"

He extended his spear to Lidia.

"Grab it and don't let go, babe!"

She did as instructed, and Juan dove for the net at the end of our skimmer. He latched onto it and became the link connecting us to Lydia, who held out her spear for Todd.

While still holding onto Kyra, the young man clamped onto the broom handle offered to him.

Even with a high probability that someone might pop an arm from their socket, they formed a human chain and swung along a wide arc to our side of the slide.

As the anchor, I dug in deep and prepared for the jolt

when our slack ran out.

Then complete chaos ensued as, one after another, the shelled creatures bombarded the group.

One narrowly missed Kyra, racing past her with its barbed cheeks flapping like a flag in the wind.

Another, lunging too far out, flipped onto its back. It twirled like a top, exposing an underside of tentacles mixed with short crustaceous legs.

It shot at the broomstick connecting Lidia to Juan, but before it could break our chain, the couple lowered the stick flush with the slide.

The thing hit it like a speed bump, sending it airborne. It landed farther down with a heavy thud and splashed into the water.

The final beast pushed itself out of the upper aqueduct but rolled on its side, spinning end over end like a hubcap thrown off a speeding tire.

When it crashed into the pool below, a wall of water shot up and a gigantic mouth breached the surface.

I don't know if the previous eel-creature was attached to this new thing or if they were two separate entities, but this sucker took up most of the pool.

With ribbons of mucus stretched between its parted lips, the humongous orifice opened wide, and a quartet of thin, black tongues lashed out like cracking bullwhips. They latched onto the shelled creatures, plucked them out of the pool, and reeled them into the pulsating maw. Then the humongous mouth clamped shut and re-submerged, once again concealing itself under the dark surface.

Back at the slide, Juan swung over and hit the wall first, followed by Lidia, then Todd, and finally, Kyra.

Each subsequent link in the chain slammed harder than the previous.

Traveling along the widest arc, Kyra took the brunt of

it. But being a gymnast, she knew how to brace for the impact, tucking her chin and turning to her side to avoid a direct hit to the head or spine.

With everyone holding fast, I maintained a firm grip on the pool skimmer to keep them in place.

"Go help," I said to Stacy. "I got this."

"You sure?"

I dug my heels in, leaned back, and tried to hide the fact I was already struggling.

"I'm good. Go."

She rushed to Juan, helping him up and off the slide. Once on stable ground, he pried his fingers loose from the skimmer and aided his wife. Stacy assisted Todd, and I ran down and pulled up Kyra.

We stumbled away from the slide and threw our arms around each other in a group hug, welcoming Stacy into the fold.

For the first time that night, I finally thought, *Okay, maybe we got this*.

Juan pulled back. "Wait. Listen. Where did everything go?"

The place was dead quiet.

"Who cares," I said. "As long as they steer clear of overflow parking."

I turned to Lydia and Juan.

"Okay. You held up your end of the deal. Now, let's get you to your boy."

THIRTY

HOLDING HANDS WITH STACY, I approached the breach in the fence. After scanning for threats and finding the coast clear, we darted out of Rapids and down the blacktop alongside The Cave.

As I led the way, Stacy asked where we were going.

I felt silly that I'd neglected to tell her earlier, but we were dealing with a ton of other issues. I quickly informed her of our promises and about getting Juan and Lidia to the overflow parking lot.

Stacy knew the exact spot and asked what the plan was for the rest of us once we got them there.

I shrugged. I assumed his abuela would take us in until things were safe again. After all we'd been through, I couldn't imagine Juan and Lidia saying, "Well, guys. It's been real," then slamming the door in our faces, leaving us out in the cold.

We finally made it to the narrow alleyway between the old-fashioned ice cream parlor and a sandwich shop.

The murky passage between the shuttered buildings was only about three feet wide. Although a tight, dark alley was the last place I wanted to venture, it was a straight shot to the back of the establishment, where a gate for deliveries opened into the employee parking lot.

I scoped out the rooftops and saw nothing waiting to ambush us. There was no canopy of webbing between the buildings where something could scuttle across or drop down from. Just a strip of clear, open sky which, nevertheless, scared the hell out of me.

"Okay," I said, pointing into the alleyway. "You guys ready?"

"Whoa-whoa! Wait!" Kyra said. Her eyes went wide and darted around. "I can't go in there! It's too tight."

"Oh, fudge," Stacy said. "We forgot. Okay, Kye. Look at me."

Kyra's eyes swam in their sockets. "It's too tight. I won't be able to breathe. I can't go in there, Stace. I can't."

"You can," Stacy said. "You got this."

"No. No, I can't! It's too tight." Kyra gasped.

Lidia rubbed her back. "Take some deep breaths, darling."

"Hey," Stacy said. "Kye, look at me."

The younger woman looked everywhere except at Stacy.

"Kyra… Hey. Kye."

Kyra finally acknowledged her.

"Close your eyes. Just take deep breaths and focus on my voice. C'mon. Close them."

Kyra complied and after Stacy started whispering something, her hitched breathing evened out.

It was amazing to see Stacy take control of the situation.

It reminded me of my mom whenever I skinned my knee as a kid.

I would charge into the house, wailing, leaking more snot and tears than blood. Mom would assess the situation in two seconds flat, then immediately go into the role of soother. She'd sit me on the counter and begin cleaning my wound while reassuring me everything was okay. Between the confidence in her eyes and the calmness in her voice, I'd realize things weren't so bad and stop crying.

If mom said it was going to be okay, then it would.

I saw those same qualities in Stacy as she comforted Kyra. If it was a practice run for what was coming down the road, Stacy was acing it.

"Now," Stacy said, "keep your eyes closed and a hand on my shoulder. Let me lead the way, Kye. Just focus on taking slow, deep breaths. Okay?"

Kyra nodded, and Stacy gestured at me to get going.

I took point and entered the alleyway first. With a hammering heart, I wondered what might be lurking behind the building, scuttling across the roof, or circling the sky above. It might be watching, waiting to attack when we stepped out back.

When the earth opened and unleashed its monstrosities, we got a rude awakening of where we now stood on the food chain. Tonight, I'd witnessed people being ripped apart and devoured. Inhaled the coppery scent of their blood and the rancid smell of their innards. I'd felt someone's intestines squash underfoot and held the cold, clammy hand of a dying friend and coworker as she was slowly being eaten alive. *Is this alleyway getting narrower?* The screams of the raccoon lady and the other guests trapped on Shock Waves suddenly echoed in my head. I'd heard the horrifying pleas from the people in the Rapids' computer room, then the tearing of their flesh and cracking of their bones. *Why is the air getting so thick? So hot and hard to breathe?* The spear in my hand felt like it weighed fifty pounds. The thick layer of sweat coating my body made my uniform cling to me. My shirt suddenly felt way too tight, especially across the chest. *Oh, shit! This alleyway* is *getting narrower!* I made a terrible mistake guiding us in here. What if the opening at the other end was just an illusion, a painting on two large sheets of plywood like an old-timey movie backdrop? And when we reached it, there'd only be an inch wide gap between the two boards that we'd never fit through. I might be able to stick my nose or mouth into the opening to suck in a little fresh air, but everyone else would keep marching forward, pinning me against the wood, crushing me. I'd suffocate. We'd all get stuck, our limbs tangled into a giant, writhing mass, shrieking and gasping for air.

Then a horde of six and eight-legged freaks would enter the alley and close in on us.

The image of baby Ryan's neon green high-top laying in the dirt flashed in my mind. The space between the walls and the tips of my shoulders was closing fast. The exit to the alley—if there even was one—never felt so far away.

My legs locked, and I stumbled.

Like the rumble of distant thunder, a voice echoed from somewhere behind me, "Are you alright?"

I gasped, raced forward, and shot out of the alleyway.

Once entering the open area behind the buildings, I collapsed against a wall, squeezed my eyes shut, and struggled to reload my lungs.

THIRTY-ONE

WHEN I OPENED MY eyes, Kyra and Juan were at the chain-link fence, messing with the gate. Todd and Lidia stood watch.

Stacy knelt next to me, brushing aside the sweaty bangs plastered to my forehead.

"I said, do you feel better?"

Apparently, I hadn't heard her the first time. Although far from okay, I nodded.

My actions were reckless. Who knew what could've been waiting on the other side? But I had to get out of there. I had never felt that way before, so I didn't know what the hell happened.

Maybe all the horrors from the night finally caught up with me.

I swallowed hard. My throat was dry and coarse like sandpaper.

"Geez, baby. You scared us. I think we were all so worried about Kyra that—"

"Oh, is she... is Kyra okay?"

"She's fine. Don't worry about her." She caressed my flushed cheek. Her touch was cool and calm. "Seriously, Danny. You okay?"

"Yeah. Fine."

"Yeah?"

"Yes." I grabbed her hand. "I love you so much."

"Love you, too."

We quickly kissed, then got back to work. The night wasn't over. It was time to get my act together and not be dead weight to the team. I might've stumbled and fallen, but I was ready to finish this.

We walked hand in hand up to the chain-link fence and stared into the dark parking lot leading to overflow.

"It's locked," Juan said, disappointed. He showed off the large padlock and thick chain sealing the gate.

I inspected the barbed wire on top of the fence and felt Juan and Lidia's glare burning a hole in my back.

So much for my great escape route.

I searched for something to drape over the wire because we were going over that fence.

Someone whistled.

We turned and saw Todd approaching with a thick furniture pad.

The blanket was draped over the top of the fence, clearing a section to climb over.

Before I could ask him where he got it, Kyra exited the backdoor of the ice cream shop with an extra broomstick spear and another pad.

"Found these in the storeroom." She handed Stacy the spear and Todd the blanket.

He threw it on top of the other one, making it two-ply.

I climbed up and over first.

After a quick check of our surroundings, I waved everyone over, helping them land safely to avoid a twisted ankle or buckled knee.

We traveled down a driveway to the beginning of the employee parking lot. A security fence ran parallel to us. Behind it was the first hill of The Long John rollercoaster, where the train plunged fifteen stories before rocketing back up the next incline.

Keeping our backs to the fence, we scanned for any threats, spotted none, then darted across the open blacktop and into the maze of cars for cover.

"Whoa. What *is* that?" Kyra asked.

I saw her staring into the park.

"Unless it's coming for us," Juan said, "I don't care."

We were about a half dozen rows in when Kyra spoke again.

"Wait! Get down-get down!"

We ducked between a Pontiac Firebird and a pickup truck parked by a lamppost.

"What?" I asked. "What is it?"

She continued peering into the park.

I followed her gaze and spotted various fires and sparking transformers. Standing awestruck, watching the park burn, it was the first time I saw the scope of the damage. The park was my place of employment, my home away from home for nearly two years, putting in grueling one-hundred-hour workweeks during the summer for overtime.

It was the place I met the love of my life.

It was also my only source of income. And now it was going up in flames. It would take months, possibly years, to inspect every structure to ensure the place was safe to reopen.

Which meant we were unemployed. And with a baby on the way, the timing could not have been worse.

Then again, we were still alive. More fortunate than most that night. So, luck had been kind to us.

"You see it?!" Kyra said.

"What?"

She pointed. "There."

"Where?"

"Under the first hill of The Long John. Right freaking in front of us."

My eyes darted up and over to the largest wooden roller coaster in the park. And right where Kyra had said, an enormous dark mass balanced on a thick crossbeam.

My mouth dropped open.

It appeared humanoid, a silhouette of a giant seated in front of the burning park. It was hunched over, almost tucked in a ball, with its head bowed like a cathedral gargoyle. The firelight rippled over the outline of its ebony skull and bony shoulders.

"What the hell is that?" Juan whispered behind us.

Lidia made the sign of the cross.

The dark figure remained motionless.

Indeed, what the hell had climbed out of the earth?

Then the giant slowly stirred, and a metamorphosis occurred.

An enormous horn sprung from the top of what I'd mistaken to be its skull, which, inexplicably, unrolled into a long, segmented tail. The appendage rose and its scythe-like tip hooked over an upper crossbeam. Its body was pulled up and flexed into a C-shape. Eight spindly legs stretched wide like splayed fingers. Gigantic pincers with serrated edges slowly lowered. Above them, a pair of powerful mantis forelegs unfolded, and a triangular head composed of bulbous eyes and twitching mandibles rose skyward. Like a piece of obsidian, it was black and glossy, broken only by oddly shaped, red patterns across its head and body.

Once unfurled, the freakish hybrid appeared to have the upper body of a praying mantis that melded into a scorpion. Hanging by its stinger, the behemoth swayed upside down.

"What the hell *is* that?" Juan repeated.

His brain must have been unable to process what we were witnessing.

"I know," I said, turning to him. "But as long as we…"

Juan's focus wasn't on the massive creature, but on the lamppost above us. More specifically, its domed light.

I glanced up, and in the firelight, saw what piqued his interest… something the size of a small dog clung to the underside of the overhanging light.

My skin crawled as the thing loosened its eight-legged grip and flipped onto the dome.

It moved so fast, and unexpectedly, Juan and I screamed in unison and jumped back.

We slammed into the Firebird and its alarm roared to life. The flashing lights and screeching horn announced our location to anything within a half-mile radius.

"What is wrong with you two?!" Lidia shouted over the alarm.

Before we could answer, the arachnid on the lamppost raised its front legs, swung down, and kicked out with its rear set, propelling itself at us.

THIRTY-TWO

JUAN AND I SCREAMED again and ducked. The jumping spider sailed over our heads and smashed through the Firebird's driver side window in an explosion of glass pellets.

Distressed by the blaring alarm, the arachnid went apeshit while trying to escape the confines of the car.

During the pandemonium, Stacy and Kyra ran to the rear of the vehicle.

Their movement caught the spider's attention.

It gave chase, scampering over the seats until slamming against the back window. Its prickly legs pawed at the glass. It snorted. Screeched. Then some kind of purple tongue unspooled from behind its large fangs and licked the window, as if trying to taste the women.

Stacy and Kyra shuddered at the unnerving sight and sounds.

"This way, y'all!" Lidia shouted.

She stood on the passenger side of the car with Todd.

As the women moved around the vehicle, the grunting spider followed them to each window until wedging itself where the dashboard and windshield met.

Once reunited with Stacy, I threw my arms around her.

"Oh, hell!" Juan said. "Big Mama is on the move. I think we got her attention!"

He pointed at the giant scorpion-mantis scrambling down the side of The Long John.

The thing paused on a set of crossbeams, cocked its head in our direction, and let off a roar that quickly tapered into the cicada chitter we heard earlier. (How a bug could roar, I'll never know. Guess we'd have to chalk it up in the same category as four-arm giant bats and trapdoor spiders the size of elephants!)

With the car alarm going off—horn honking, lights flashing, and a screeching spider stuck inside—the spectacle drew the gigantic beast directly to us.

We took off racing down an aisle of vehicles, with me taking the lead.

A loud crash sounded behind us.

The creature flattened The Long John's perimeter fence, stomping it into the asphalt.

Now at ground level, the hybrid was much larger than I initially thought, easily the size of a tractor trailer.

While I kept glancing behind us, everyone else's focus remained ahead.

Without slowing in its pursuit, the behemoth slammed one of its mighty pincers down on the honking Firebird, crushing both the vehicle and the screeching spider inside. The alarm petered out of tune and went silent as the beast blew past it.

"Move your ass, sport!" Juan yelled from the rear.

Whipping back ahead, I caught movement in my periphery.

It was another spider flying at us.

"Look out!" I yelled and raised my spear.

I intended to knock the crap out of it like a piñata. Instead, I impaled it.

The creature's inertia ripped the broomstick out of my hands as if opening an umbrella in a windstorm. The shishkebabbed spider flew over the car beside us, vanishing with my spear.

Thrown off course, I clipped a side mirror, pinballed into a truck, and spilled onto the driveway parallel to our path.

"Oh, my gosh," Stacy said. "Are you okay?"

Although slightly dazed, I sat up, nodded, and grunted. Numerous hands yanked me to my feet.

"I got him," Stacy said. "Go! Go! Go!" she told everyone.

Grabbing my hand, she led me away.

The remaining group split into pairs and raced down separate aisles in a mad dash for the wooded area at the back of the parking lot. Juan and Lidia ran in the aisle to our left. Kyra and Todd to our right.

The trees were within sight, but we still had at least a dozen rows to go.

We continued racing along the individual aisles when the sound of crunching metal and shattered glass rose behind us. Stacy and I flinched and ducked but kept moving.

I looked over my shoulder and saw the giant running on top of the cars. Under its massive weight, roofs caved in, side windows blew out, and windshields spider-webbed and crumpled.

Backlit by the burning park, the creature was a flurry of stampeding legs. Its thorax puffed up and the tip of its stinger curled over its body. Both its Z-shaped forelegs and pincers snapped open, ready to snatch us up once we were within reach.

Stacy yanked my hand to pick up the pace.

Even while pushing my legs to their extreme, I couldn't help but continuously peek over my shoulder.

With each thunderous crash of metal and glass, the behemoth was closing the distance between us.

Approaching a car, I glimpsed a group of people hiding inside. I lurched away, not expecting to see terrified faces staring back at us.

They were in the direct path of the oncoming beast and were seconds from being crushed.

Stacy and I only had enough time to pound the windows and yell, "Look out!" "It's coming!" before we blew past.

Glancing back, I saw five teenagers— four guys and a girl—scrambling out of the car before it got squashed.

The group only made it a few steps into their escape when the scorpion-mantis attacked, striking all at once with lethal precision.

The first guy was snipped in two at the waist by a pincer. His upper body popped up like a top while his lower half dropped and spilled out a steaming pile of intestines.

The other pincer swung wide and swiped the girl into the side of a van, popping her like a water balloon. The force of the impact rocked the van and sent a crimson explosion into the air that drenched the surrounding vehicles.

A few cars over, the mantis foreleg struck like a lightning bolt and skewered another guy, entering his screaming mouth and exiting between his twitching legs.

Farther back, the scorpion tail punched its stinger through the fourth teen and flung him to the other side of the parking lot.

The final guy got plucked up by the mantis forelegs and had his head and shoulders bitten off by chomping mandibles.

The entire massacre lasted only a few seconds, but temporarily pulled the creature's attention off us while it fed.

Our good fortune didn't last long.

A few cars ahead, a large shadowy mass dropped from a lamppost and blocked our path.

We skidded to a halt, and Stacy raised her spear at the crouching spider.

Failing to notice that we had stopped, the rest of the group kept going.

Now on our own, we stared down the lesser of two threats, steeling ourselves to charge the spider.

"Okay," Stacy said. "You ready?"

I snapped off an antenna from the station wagon next to us and sized it up. "Yep!"

Before we could advance, the arachnid squealed and fled the scene, getting far away from the juggernaut resuming its pursuit of us.

Stacy bolted forward with me in tow.

Eyeing the dark cluster of trees ahead, I hoped their leafy canopy would provide enough cover to race in, scale the wall, and slink through the neighborhood to seek shelter elsewhere. I also prayed there wouldn't be anything lurking in the woods. If so, we were running at a full sprint toward it.

The destruction grew louder over our shoulders.

I peeked back.

The thing roared and scuttled over vehicles, caving them in, popping their tires. Its bloodstained, serrated pincers and forelegs snapped open, welcoming us.

The other couples—still unaware that we'd fallen behind—barreled into the tree line ahead of us. I checked our distance from the charging creature.

We weren't going to make it.

"Don't look back!" Stacy yelled and pulled my hand again.

The giant was gaining on us. I whipped my head forward and focused solely on Stacy as she led me through a seemingly endless aisle of cars.

This was it. There was no way we were going to outrun

the thing before making it to the tree line.

We fought all night, beating the odds at every turn. But this, *this* was it.

"I love you!" I screamed. I wanted her to know it, especially if they might be the last words out of my mouth and the final ones she'd hear. "I love you so much, Stacy!"

She gripped my hand tighter. "Don't! You tell me that later! Just move your goddamn ass!"

Vehicles we'd blown past only seconds earlier were trampled under the giant's steps. Car windshields splintered and folded. Pellets of glass rained over the area.

The beast's massive forelegs shot down and speared the cars flanking us. One punctured the front quarter panel of a Honda Civic, popping its tire in an ear-piercing explosion of dust and shards of rubber, while the other impaled the engine block of a Ford Mustang.

We screamed, yet never slowed, pushing our legs to their breaking point.

The creature roared and ripped one foreleg loose.

Fighting to pull free from the Mustang's engine, its pincers hoisted the car into the air, then slammed the vehicle down, releasing its trapped limb.

The failed attack bought us precious seconds on our escape.

We rocketed out of the last row of cars, leaping off the asphalt and into the dirt, when something huge shot down from the heavens and speared the earth. Then it whipped back up, sending an explosion of mud and dirt clods into the air.

I peeked back and saw the monster winding up its tail for another strike.

Panic and exhaustion strangled the air from my lungs. We hit the low-hanging trees, weaving around their thick trunks, trying to put as many obstacles between us and the creature as possible.

A dozen trees in, we hid behind a large oak to catch our breath, then peeked out and quickly ducked back.

The thing crouched at the edge of the lot.

It seemed reluctant to enter and risk getting snared in the thick branches.

We should've made a run for the fence. Instead, we stayed put.

Watched.

Waited.

Too afraid to move.

THIRTY-THREE

THE BEAST HOVERED OVER the ground. Its bulbous eyes darted back and forth, seeking our slightest movement. It paused, then studied the limbs above. I hoped it realized it was too large to enter and move on.

Instead, its enormous forelegs and pincers snapped open and sliced the air.

Wood splintered. Branches and leaves rained down.

To my horror, it was pruning the trees to make room to squeeze through. As proof, the creature's poisonous tail lowered, aligning with its body for easier access under the branches.

After clearing a path, it slid forward and went to work on the next row of trees.

We had to get out of there. Now.

"Yo! Danny-boy!" Juan screamed from somewhere behind us.

Straddling the top of the brick wall and pounding his chest like Kong, he waved us over with an enormous grin.

I think the night finally broke the poor bastard.

Stacy snatched my hand, and we darted for the wall.

The behemoth spotted us and sprung forward. Its tail curled to strike but got tangled in the dense canopy of foliage.

It struggled to free itself, twisting onto its back to hack

and slash at the tree limbs restraining it.

Once at the wall, Juan grabbed Stacy's arm. I lifted her hips, and she went up and over.

Behind me, the thing whipped itself into a frenzy while trying to break free. Branches swayed and snapped. The cascading leaves were so thick it looked like a ticker tape parade.

Gawking like an idiot at the spectacle, I gasped when Juan grabbed me by the shirt. Only his head and shoulders were now visible over the fence.

"C'mon, brother! Got a big surprise for ya over here!"

He struggled to pull me up.

Then, from out of the darkness, more hands reached down and ripped me off my feet.

Once atop the fence, I saw a half dozen soldiers on the other side. Those who weren't helping me were providing cover with machine guns.

Overwhelmed by the sight, the air rushed from my lungs.

A soldier motioned to the ladder below and I quickly descended.

Stacy and I were wrapped in blankets and whisked down a residential street to join the others from our group. As we moved along, something materialized out of the dark. Something big. I saw the tank turret and smiled.

"I know! Right?!" Juan slapped my shoulder and chortled. "Thank God this town's got an armory, huh?"

We were escorted through an intersection filled with military Jeeps and transport trucks. Soldiers spilled out of the vehicles, some carrying shoulder-fired missiles.

Once reunited with Lydia, Todd, and Kyra, we traveled another block, past a second perimeter. Beyond it, the neighborhood residents stood on their front porches and lawns. They clutched shotguns, deer rifles, and pistols.

The neighbors waved at us and continued eyeing the hotspot down the street. They were ready to provide backup, to protect homestead and property against trespassers, whether it be two, four, six, eight-legged or other.

Unable to accept that we were finally out of harm's way, I kept checking behind us. The scorpion-mantis was still on the other side of the wall, probably freed by now. But a ton of well-armed soldiers were between us and it, which made me feel slightly better.

Nevertheless, it was still too close for comfort.

"Hostile!" someone yelled. "Twelve o'clock!"

"There! In the trees above the fence!"

We spun and stared at the far end of the street from which we came. My stomach constricted.

A spotlight blasted the trees.

The overhanging branches rustled and bulged. Then a mantis head burst out of the treetops.

The beast sprung forward with a roar.

"Fire!" a soldier roared back.

Machine guns with red-hot tracers riddled the creature, followed by thunderous explosions of heavy artillery.

We all jumped and ran for cover. It wasn't our fight anymore. I clutched Stacy's hand, and she grabbed Kyra's, who reached out for Todd's.

Juan and Lidia waved us closer.

"Abuelita's is two streets down," he said. "C'mon!"

Over the fiery engagement, I yelled to Stacy, "Should we be leaving like this?"

"What?!"

The gunfire and explosions were ear-splitting.

"The Army... or National Guard... don't you think they'll want to talk to us? Find out what we know?"

"I think they're busy right now! We'll come back later!"

Kyra jumped in and shouted, "Yeah, Danny! You

promised to get Juan and Lidia to their son! That means we don't stop until you accomplish that!"

I smiled and pointed at her as if to say, '*You rock!*'

Once we made it two blocks over, the sounds of battle ceased. Then the soldiers cheered.

Hearing their victory gave me the first real sense of security.

Minutes later, we witnessed Juan and Lidia's tearful reunion with their little boy and grandma.

The sight of it filled my heart with hope.

After all the hell we went through to get to that moment, it proved we were strong enough for whatever was thrown our way. And that any future struggle would probably pale in comparison to what we faced and overcame that night together.

THIRTY-FOUR

NEWS REPORTS HAD YET to reveal exactly where in the earth the things were living or how a routine construction site opened Pandora's box.

Although all the creatures—both in and outside the park—were supposedly killed, their remains were being studied by various government agencies to determine possible origins, as well as classifying new species and mutations.

They tried to assure us that we were safe, but how could they say that when they didn't even know those things were down there in the first place?

Or did they?

Three months had passed since that terrifying night. The park remained closed indefinitely. Stacy, Kyra, and I all got jobs at the mall. After working outside for so long, being constantly indoors was kind of weird, but I was looking forward to summers with air-conditioning.

Stacy was hired as a sales associate at Waldenbooks, Kyra worked at Musicland, and I sold bomber jackets and other apparel at Wilsons Leather.

We always scheduled our breaks at the same time so we could eat together at the food court.

Todd hung out daily at the mall and always joined us on our break. His mom dropped him off after school and he'd cruise around the different stores, usually spending most of his time at Kyra's. He claimed it was to check out the new releases at their listening station by the front counter where she worked. But they only played the latest pop and new wave cassettes. With Todd being a total headbanger, we think it had more to do with some secret crush on Kyra and just wanting to be around her more. There was no other reason he'd endure repeat listenings of Billy Ocean's "Get Outta of My Dreams, Get Into My Car" or Phil Collins's "Groovy Kind of Love."

When I asked him about it, he just smiled and looked away, which confirmed he must have his own groovy kind of love for Kyra.

As for Juan and Lidia, we talk pretty much every other day.

They (along with Todd, of course) join us in cheering on Kyra at her various gymnastic meets.

Although Stacy's barely showing in her belly, we're constantly asking Lidia and Juan baby questions and for their parenting advice.

They've happily accepted the role of big brother and sister, but I think they have no idea what they've signed on for once the kid is born and we're freaking out over every little thing. I hope they're ready for our panicked calls at all hours of the night.

After Stacy and I turned eighteen (me in November, she in early December), we moved into an efficiency apartment. It's tiny, but it's home.

She's been seeing a doctor. So far, everything is going

great. We told the doc not to tell us the baby's sex. Let it be a surprise.

Speaking of surprises... we broke the news to our parents about the pregnancy. As expected, my mom took it much better than her mom and dad, hardcore Catholics who frown upon the whole premarital sex thing.

But they'll come around.

To help ease a little of that pressure, I bought an engagement ring to make things legit. It's kind of pathetic looking but, given our circumstances, it's the best I could afford.

I'm still trying to figure out how I'm going to propose. It needs to be romantic and memorable, because Stacy deserves nothing but the best.

EPILOGUE

ABOUT A MONTH LATER, just after the New Year, Juan called me in a panic. He was doing yard work at his abuela's when he spotted something unusual.

"Danny-boy, I need you to get over here and look at something. Now."

When Stacy and I pulled up, he was alone, standing at the far end of the driveway in front of the detached garage. He had an ax in one hand and a box of matches in the other. A jerry can of gasoline and a fire extinguisher sat at his feet.

We got out of the car and rushed over.

"What's the matter?" Stacy asked.

"Yeah, man. What is it?"

"I was raking leaves over there when I saw it." He pointed to a grass strip between the garage and fence, where a rake lay abandoned by a large stack of firewood.

"Saw what?"

"Go look and tell me what you think it is. Tell me I'm not being paranoid so I can call the cops."

Stacy and I glanced at each other, then at the ax, matches, and gasoline. We hadn't seen Juan look this frightened since *that* night. And it scared the hell out of us.

My stomach suddenly got that familiar sinking feeling.

"Go take a look. It's safe... for now. I just want a second opinion."

"All right. I'll go."

I breathed deeply and motioned to Stacy that there was probably nothing to worry about.

I slowly entered the narrow walkway and peeked behind the woodpile.

"Whoa, Jesus!" I said, briskly walking back to them.

Juan nodded. "Yeah. So, I'm not crazy? And if it's here, there could be more in the neighborhood."

"More of what?" Stacy asked.

My throat was too dry, too tight, to answer.

"You guys go inside and call the cops. Mi abuela is napping in her room, so use the phone in the kitchen. Keep it low. I don't want her panicking." He picked up the gasoline can. "I'll stay here and keep watch."

Stacy shook her head. "What? What is it?" When I still couldn't answer, she stepped forward to see for herself.

"No!" I took her arm, gently pulled her back, and placed my hand over her baby bump. "C'mon, Stace. Come with me. Please."

Upon entering the house, she demanded to know what was behind the woodpile.

I paused and stared at her.

"Eggs."

Stacy grew pale.

"Hey, babe," I said. "There's nothing to worry about. Everything will be fine. I promise."

Then I squeezed her hand so she wouldn't feel mine as it began to tremble.

MATT KURTZ'S
SHOCK WAVES

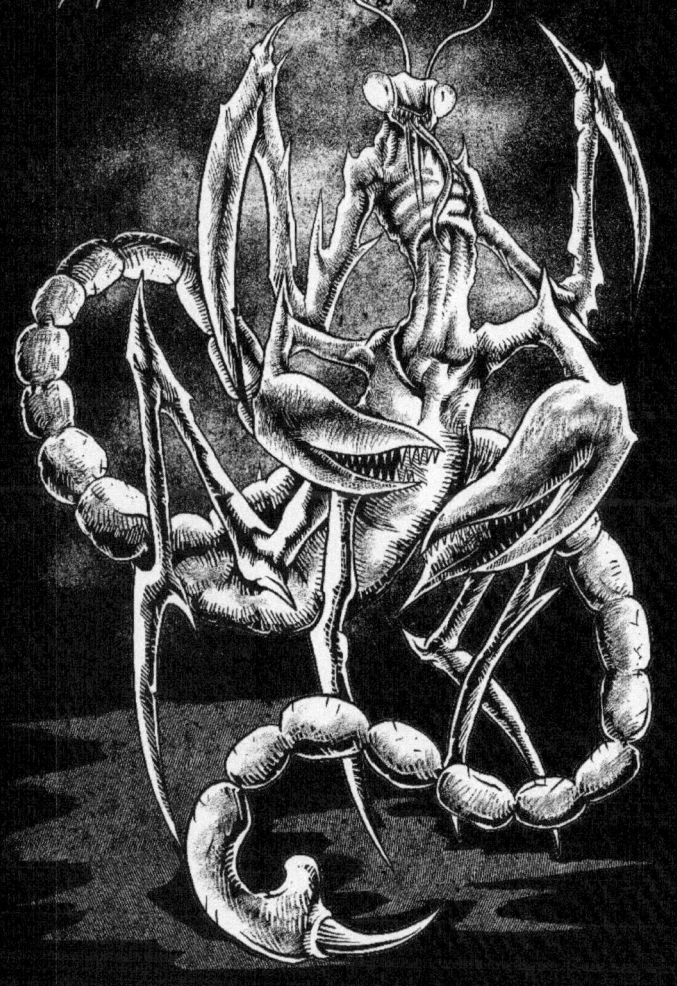

SINCE THIS STORY TAKES place in the '80s—and the Eighties were all about cool soundtracks—the following would've been on its (dream) soundtrack if it had been made into a movie:

Danny and Stacy's Mix Tape

"Think I'm in Love" - Eddie Money
"Caught Up In You" - 38 Special
"Rain" - The Cult
"House of Pain" - Faster Pussycat
"Round and Round" - Ratt
"Pictures of You" - The Cure
"Miles Away" - Winger
"Love Gun" - KISS
"Angel" - Aerosmith
"Stripped" - Depeche Mode
"Walk in the Shadows" - Queensrÿche
"Stand Back" - Stevie Nicks
"Hunting High and Low" - A-Ha
"When Love and Hate Collide" - Def Leppard*

NOTE: As with most songs from the '80s, a lot of these are about breaking up, which really doesn't apply to *Shock Waves*. They were just songs I jammed to while writing this tale, helping to bring me back in time (the way only a song can.)

*Although this was released after the events in the book, Joe Elliot's vocals make it the ultimate power ballad. It must be included, timeline be damned.

ABOUT THE AUTHOR

MATT KURTZ CONSIDERS THIS book somewhat autobiographical. Aside from any construction site explosions, teenage pregnancies, or giant things coming out of the ground to eat people, he did work as a ride foreman at an amusement park during his mid to late teens.

His other books include the witchcraft creep-fest, *The Rotting Within*, and *Kinfolk*, a criminals vs cannibals horror/thriller. (Both novels were published by Grindhouse Press.) If you're looking for bite-sized horrors, he also has a three-volume collection of short stories.

Find more about him (or contact him) at the following:

Twitter and Instagram - @MattKurtzWrites
Facebook - Matt Kurtz
MattKurtzWrites.com

His books can be found on Amazon. If you're interested in buying a signed copy, feel free to send him a direct message using any of the above social media platforms.

Matt resides somewhere in Texas, where he's working on his next tale.

Printed in Great Britain
by Amazon